Commune of the Golden Sun

Miriam Sagan

Cholla Needles Arts & Literary Library
Joshua Tree, California

Cover art by Gordon Johnson and Kevin McIver
Author photo by Matt Morrow
Thanks to Devon Miller-Duggan
and Isabel Wison-Sagan for
being both alpha and beta readers.
And to Richard Feldman for pretty much everything.

https://www.chollaneedles.com

Copyright © 2024 Miriam Sagan
All rights reserved.
ISBN: 9798864210833

The Old Tale

Once upon a time, long ago, in ancient China, there were two children—a boy and a girl—who were inseparable. They played together all day long and loved each other.

Once they overheard their mothers remarking on this and thought that the mothers had said they were betrothed.

But when they grew up, the young woman, whose name was Chen, was engaged by her family to an older, wealthy man. In despair, the young man decided to leave the village and go to the city, taking his boat down the river. As he was preparing to go, he saw a figure running towards him in the morning mist. It was Chen, and she shouted, "Wait! It's me!"

They poled the flat-bottomed boat out of the reeds and left the bank for the current flowing downstream. They arrived in the city and learned its ways. There they got married, found a house, and had children.

But the man, now fully grown, was haunted by how unfilial his behavior had been. He felt the need to apologize to Chen's family. So, they got in the boat and went back, poling against the current, helped by the wind in a small sail. When they arrived, the man bowed to Chen's now-aged parents and apologized for taking her away against their wishes.

They were shocked. "But Chen has been here all along!" they exclaimed. "She is sick in bed and cannot speak, but she can understand what is said to her."

At that moment, the pale, transparent form of Chen-in-bed got up and walked towards the woman who had left and then returned. They merged into one person.

The Zen Master Turns This Into A Koan
By Asking One Question:

Which is the real Chen?

Maira, 2026-2056

She was still so little back then. She'd point and say—"moon." If she said "salt," she'd add "pepper." Everything was in pairs—she liked that—including the two of us.

She could say "rain," because I used to take her to one of the ruined fake places, the indoor arcade where it still rained from the painted ceiling four times an hour. There were no longer lights, so the sky didn't darken before the storm, but it still rained faithfully on the quarter hour.

We'd sit for a long time, looking at the white clouds painted motionless on the false sky. They looked real, sometimes more real than the actual sky, which burned week after week without precipitation.

Of course, Vegas was always dry. It was the desert, after all. I'd lived there my whole life, and I was used to it: the way my bare feet had cracks in the soles, the way my hair never curled. But this was even dryer than that. The electrical grid was constantly stressed. The AC and the lights would go out, then come back on. And I couldn't help wondering if the day would come when nothing would light up again.

The Colorado River was dry, the reservoirs so low that every little town or ranch or ancient ruin it had drowned was now exposed again to sunlight. My mother used to say: someday we'll turn on a water faucet and sand will pour out. She was dead before that seemed like a real possibility, before I realized she hasn't been exaggerating.

We were going to have to go. I knew that. I was just putting it off. There was still plenty to eat. I'd stored up, and the looters union had hundreds of stalls at the market. It would be years before we starved. But that wasn't a plan.

The Strip was eerie. Sometimes it was lit up but half empty. More frighteningly, sometimes it was dark. I never expected to see stars above Vegas. And now I saw them, shining brightly and seemingly close at hand through the dry atmosphere. People had stopped visiting, even stopped gambling. They'd gambled my whole life until now, through every crisis, through pandemics and disrupted elections, through violence and weakened supply lines. But things were getting worse. Hospitals and churches had emergency generators, with basements and corridors open to the homeless and to anyone who couldn't manage alone.

I kept thinking I could manage. After all, that was the central belief I had been raised with: we can manage. My mother clung to that even during the times when it hardly seemed true.

And we loved each other, me and my tiny girl. We were all the other person had in this world—and that was fine with me. She was two years old. I was thirty-two, without a man.

The last of the big fights with Jake had turned into *the* big fight. We were getting on each other's nerves, the three of us crammed into a one-bedroom garden apartment. At least the windows opened, and we ran fans at night. No internet. No work. No hope about what was going to come next.

"I'm going to Golden Sun," he said.

"Back to that commune? But how? It's a thousand miles east of Vegas. Is there gas? Can the car possibly...."

He glared at me. "You think things are going to get

better? The Tyrant has banned elections. He's President for Life. Don't you think they're building concentration camps. And besides, it's only about 700 miles." He drove me crazy with comments like that, always reminding me that he had been a math teacher.

"Maybe. Maybe it will get better. I can manage," I said.

"Oh, come off it, Maira. Things are a disaster."

"Maybe," I repeated. I couldn't really disagree with him, but then again, I didn't want to agree.

"I'm going. And you'd better come. For the child's sake."

"Touch either of us and I'll slit your throat when you sleep." I surprised even myself.

This wasn't the way I usually talked, but of course it was a lot like my mother. She'd died when I was twenty, but that was not the last of her. Usually she slept inside me, exhausted and washed-up. But now she was awake, almost sober, and ready to fight.

"Maira," he said softly. "We used to be friends. We used to be lovers. I care about you. I love the girl. She's mine too."

"I'll kill you," I said. So he left.

Months passed in the desert without rain. No summer monsoon. No winter storms. People were strange wherever I went—either rude or furtive. They crashed into me on the sidewalk and didn't apologize. It was as if no one knew where they were going. I held Tessa's hand tightly, but I was nervous all the time. I began to see that Jake was right. Well, if I was honest I'd always known that. Let's just say I was now admitting it to myself.

And he sent me three postcards. The U.S. mail was still delivered a few times a week. Mine was mostly just junk and bills. But suddenly there were postcards. The image was the same on each one: WELCOME TO LAS VEGAS emblazoned in neon yellow on a scene that was now in the past, the skyline of the city lit up and blazing against the dark.

The first said: "At night I met a man on one of the east forks of the Little Colorado, on a pebble wash. We wrestled till dawn. And I hurt my leg and have a bad limp."

The second said: "Golden is as we left it. Quarrelsome, and too many cats. The old crew is mostly still here. And the food is good as always, even the kale."

The third said: "Maira, you and the child better come. I'm Black, you're white. I'm a man, you're a woman. We don't have to be together. Bring the child. I'm hearing rumors. It's less than a three-day hitchhike. P.S. Put on some lipstick and bring your knife."

It turned out that I didn't really need either the makeup or the blade. We got picked up right away by a single mom with two kids in the back. Both older than my Tessa, and they played with her for hours and fed her all kinds of things we didn't normally eat—candy, chips. She adored them and for months after asked about the "big kids" in the car. The mom didn't offer much in the way of conversation. She was a good driver, and I navigated with the paper map in my lap. After the cell networks went down, I was glad I knew how to read an atlas. I'd taught myself as a child, trying to figure out the globe and where we were on it.

The highway was more desolate than usual. There were a lot fewer trucks on I-40. A few years before it was just one big rig after another, whizzing by. Now you could go for miles with very little traffic. The rest stops were closed, as were the visitors' centers at the state lines. The signs were still there: Welcome to Arizona. And all those places that were fun to visit—tourist traps that sold cheap turquoise and beer and that advertised clean restrooms and two-headed dinosaurs—were shut as well. Some were boarded over, and a few that I glimpsed looked like they might have been trashed.

Eventually the mom needed to sleep, and I took the wheel as far as Flagstaff. She was carrying extra gas. She didn't explain, but I could see she was afraid to stop. I wondered if it would be easier or safer to get off the interstate and shunpike for a while, but it wasn't my place to suggest that. We were just hitchhiking.

The rules were up to the mom. If anyone needed to pee, we just pulled onto the shoulder of the highway and told the kids "Make it quick!" We did pass a bunch of abandoned cars, and a few times we saw fires burning out in the fields. But traffic remained light. It wasn't like that old classic *Mad Max* or anything. Still, it made me realize that Jake had been right. It really was time to leave Vegas.

Tessa and I got out east of Flag, aiming to go south. The landscape was familiar enough. I'd been this way before with Jake. Our next ride was with two girls—maybe sisters, or lovers—something. They went out of their way for us. It seemed like women were keeping out an eye for each other on the road. I'd never seen anyone actually drive on the amount of pot they were eating, but they could do it. Stoned girls were less frightening to me than any man—drunk or sober.

I've always had a thing about rearview mirrors. Like I imagine I can really see the past in them, things receding as I drive away. But when I leaned to peer in the mirror all I saw was myself looking a bit pinched and worried. Tessa was asleep beside me, wrapped in her own arms. The two girls in front were humming something wordlessly, then starting to giggle and cutting off abruptly as if there was nothing to laugh about.

For a moment I imagined I saw Vegas in the rear view, receding into the past. A place where real palm trees looked fake and fake ones looked real. A place where I had been what I considered to be my real self, up until now.

The stoned girls dropped us on the county road, part of a rural grid that crossed now-unused agricultural land and flat, wild fields. I knew where I was. It was late afternoon, and we were essentially at the bottom of the long dirt driveway into Golden. They offered to take us in, but I didn't think that was a good idea. I wasn't sure I remembered how the wards worked, or if the place was even protected that way anymore. They went off waving good-bye. Tessa blew a kiss on her fist, and waved too. She was a small figure standing in the dust of a mesa covered in juniper and piñon. I took her hand, and we started walking in.

It was quiet except for some jays calling out raucously. Three turkey vultures flew above us, riding the thermals. "Caw, caw," Tessa said. She didn't know many birds, just crows and mourning doves. The air had a quality I remembered from my previous visit—soft, almost tangible. It seemed to shimmer as we went forward. I kept an eye out for the wards. The last time I'd been here—more than a half dozen years ago—bones and wind chimes made of twisted metal bits had hung in the trees. Sometimes—spookily—a small dead animal or a snakeskin. Even then Golden had wanted to keep people out.

That was my first and last visit to Golden with Jake.

He'd wanted to show it off to me at the start of our relationship, show me his special place. It hadn't really grabbed me, though, not the way it did Jake. It was quite pleasant, with a lovely swimming hole from underground springs. And each person had his or her own room, a cozy bit of privacy. The food was great—fresh and varied. It seemed like almost everyone there could cook and did a good job. People showed off with curries and stir fries and fancy stews. There was a lot of baking. I had to agree with Jake that it was the best pie I'd ever eaten: blueberry, strawberry, apple rhubarb, and a lot more.

But I liked Vegas: the Strip, the pulse, the quieter neighborhoods where people knew each other. I had no desire to leave, not then. Besides, I'd been born there. And to be born there, as my mother often reminded me, was to see the swirling dice that most people ignored. Gamblers shook and expected to win. They kept on expecting that, no matter how life turned out. But I knew I was taking a chance every time I walked out my front door, kissed someone, quit a job, or had a baby. Or decided to hitchhike east just in case the apocalypse really had arrived.

On that first visit to Golden, Jake had said the whole thing about wards was made up. Kitchen magic, low-rent hoodoo, cooked up by witchy women to scare strangers. Still, at Golden people had told me—don't just come in, wait to be greeted, you can get…well, burned, or shocked or something.

There was no sign of anything like this, though, as Tessa and I walked along. And then I saw what I was looking for—the old cracked wooden sign, painted with a picture of a naked child riding a horse while solar rays streamed behind. And the words, faded but legible. COMMUNE OF THE GOLDEN SUN.

"Baby," Tessa said, pointing to the naked child. From the sign to the first outbuilding would be less than a mile. Tessa was a good walker, humming a bit of a made-up snatch of song to herself. Suddenly I was hit with a memory, not of Golden but of my own mother, humming over the dishes. My mother Mel had once been beautiful, but by the time I came along she was almost forty—washed up, angry, and broke. She'd gone from chorus girl to croupier. It paid, and she had a little bungalow house she shared with her on-again, off-again girlfriend Cherise. It paid, but she was on her feet all shift, her back was a wreck from a hit and run, and what was left of her soul was neither bad nor good. Not great for a child.

"Mommy, look." Tessa pointed. There was the first group of buildings. I led her towards the dining hall. There was a meeting going on. Several dozen adults, brightly dressed with outlandish dyed hairdos, beards, scarves. They looked like a pretty flock of birds but their faces were angry—some furious, some withdrawn. It was one of Golden's infamous, no doubt interminable, meetings.

"There's a precedent," said a man with a drooping mustache.

"Fuck you and your precedent," a woman retorted. "This is a real problem, do you get that. Real? As in reality. Not some made-up bullshit."

"No abusive talk, please," a different woman said, adjusting her flowing shawl. "And please talk in turn. Where is the talking stick? Would someone pass it around? Thank you. This meeting really needs to get under control."

I hesitated at the threshold. After three seconds of this, I was already annoyed and stupefied. But then Tessa saw something just outside. Children—naked, wild, playing.

"Mommy...."

"It's OK. You can go," I told her. That was the first time I saw her really run away from me, towards something else. She did not look back. Was that the start of it all? Should I blame Golden for taking her from me? Not really, because she left Golden too. Also without looking back. Golden was good for her at first. She had real friends and grown-ups who cared. There was always someone to bandage a knee or answer a question.

Golden was far better for Tessa than life with a single mom in an apartment in an apocalypse.

Despite the annoying meetings, Golden was mostly a peaceful place. Kids didn't hit each other. And no adult would ever hit a child or even use a disrespectful tone. There was dress-up and dancing in the rain and swimming and hiking and endless pretend. Jake was sure that this better way of life would create happy adults out of free children.

That day we arrived, I was greeted warmly.

"Maira!" The woman with the shawl from the meeting ran over. "You're here! Jake will be so relieved. I hear it is terrible out there."

"Pretty bad," I had to admit.

"Thank goodness you arrived safely. And there's your daughter. Tessa, right? She's adorable. She's already fitting in."

"I'm glad to be here," I said, slightly surprising myself. She embraced me. "We're glad you are too."

The truth was, I felt more relaxed at Golden than I had been in a long time. Golden had been founded in the last century as part of the back-to-the-land hippie movement. The founders were idealists, egalitarians. Dozens of communes had sprung up in the counterculture seemingly overnight, like mushrooms. And then died off just as quickly. But Golden had survived for almost a hundred years for one simple reason: money.

An early enthusiastic member had been the grandson of a man who had invented something, a small but necessary part of oil drilling. The grandson held the patent, at that time probably worth millions. When the grandson had died young of leukemia, he had been buried in the pretty cemetery beneath Pook's Hill, which overlooked the property. And left the patent to Golden.

It had kept them afloat for years. Jake had told me all this and even described the widget in his usual professorial manner. I paid no attention to the widget, but I did understand about the money, which was held in common.

"Doesn't Golden feel bad about profiting from fossil fuels? Polluting the earth and all that?" I asked.

Jake had laughed. "You'd fit right in there, Maira,"

he'd said. "They've been quibbling about that for years."

Perhaps there was some guilt, as Golden emphasized ecology and also pacifism. So of course it had never imagined that it was raising its children to be soldiers. It was raising farmers and mechanics and cooks and bakers and healers. And I myself could never have imagined that Tessa would vanish and despite her nonviolent upbringing would kill or be killed.

But no one can see the future. Sometimes I think I can't even really see the past. If we'd stayed in Vegas, most likely Tessa and I would have died early on in the war.

Golden was safer in many ways. Really, although I never told him, I knew that Jake had probably saved our lives.

Golden was more than just a hippie commune. It had shared beliefs that kept the group together. Everyone was supposedly equal, which of course wasn't true. The beautiful, the sexy, the tough-assed, the bossy, the noisy... these people tended to lead. The folks who lived there seemed to just take the place for granted, as if Golden was normal. But actually it had taken thought and effort to have created it. It took the same to keep it going.

And yes, you did need some rules for more than a hundred and twenty people to live together and depend on each other, day in and day out. I can't say I truly trusted that, although the rules themselves were excellent. No violence. No stealing. No slacking off on the work roster. It was certainly a pleasanter life than most people led working for the man and commuting in traffic.

I loved the climate—hot in summer, some snow in winter, but always sunshine and clear skies. And as Jake always said, there was always someone to talk to, someone to hang out with. You were never lonely. It was just that...well, groups of people have never been my favorite thing. At least I had my own room. I'd never have managed without that.

At Golden, the generations of children lived in nests. Those born within a year or two of each other naturally fell in together. When they got to be old enough they were given a little outbuilding to live in as they pleased. By the time they were six or seven they had a full roster of chores—the fields, the animals, cooking prep, cleanup. And what was called "school"—the basics, in a minimal and haphazard fashion, which wouldn't have passed muster even in the freest of free schools in the outside world. At least everyone learned to read and write—sort of.

But it was obviously paradise for children. They could hang out all day by the small spring-fed pond, very unusual for that desert terrain. And the goats. Tessa loved the goats, although she started off afraid of the beady-eyed chickens. But in a few months, she was indistinguishable from a child born and raised at Golden. And she had friends, in particular the little clique of the Four, lively girls about her age. The four who would betray us and break our hearts.

"Golden sits in basin land. It almost touches an alluvial plain on the east side of the mountains. There are mountains and narrow canyons. The strata are of limestone, gypsum, shale, sandstone. To the far south, the Jornada del Muerto—the Journey of the Dead Man, obviously a waterless badlands."

Jake was droning on to me in his professor voice,

about things I neither knew nor cared about. But I tried to look attentive. Maybe we'd get back together. It would be good for Tessa. And although Golden was full of fit, bearded guys working on machinery, none of them really attracted me.

"Listen Maira. This is fascinating. I've got a National Park Service pamphlet here from the 1940s. It says: The ruins of two ancient Indian pueblos and Spanish missions are situated in the Gran Quivira quadrangle. The following brief notes are inserted as a matter of general interest. About the time the Pilgrims were landing at Plymouth Rock, Spanish padres in the Southwest were constructing Gran Quivira Mission to serve the surrounding 10 cities of the Jumano Indians. The older church is badly disintegrated, but the massive walls of the second church and its attached monastery and convent, on which work began about 1649, are still standing. The latter church probably was abandoned about 1670. Also included in the monument are ruined pueblos."

"It sounds sad," I said. "Basically, those people were conquered. Probably wiped out." I knew Jake would like my observations. After all, I'd learned to talk that way from him.

"Yeah, it does. Still, it would be interesting to see the place."

I inched close to Jake. Dusk was falling, an intimate time of day. Most of those guys were in couples. They'd like an outside woman, but that wasn't going to work for me. The truly single guys, well, there were obvious reasons they were single.

But Jake was still talking. "You know, people were on this land for thousands of years before those missions. Hunting and gathering. There was rice grass out here, as tall as we are. Before cattle came, and overgrazing, which cut those arroyos. You can find the camps sometimes. I found a beautiful scraper for hide. Just perfect for a woman's hand. With some glittery red specks on it, like for decoration. Someone so long ago took the trouble...."

I took his hand. We knew each other well. The pressure of my fingers said everything I needed to say.

It didn't last that time either, but it was fun while it lasted. Until it stopped being fun in an all-too-familiar way.

I'm old now. I don't mind that word; in fact I'm proud of it. I'm much older than my mother was when she died. I go about my business, and people seem to respect and even like me. After all, I've been here a long time; I'm an elder. I was one of the group that shut Golden to the outside world, that sealed us off from so much war and hate. And contagion, let's not forget that. The world was dying. I'm pretty much sure it still is, but a slow death. After Tessa and the rest of the Four left, we couldn't afford to lose any more.

You can no longer hitchhike to Golden, walk the road, and be greeted with a hot meal. You can no longer leave and return with tales of how Golden is far better than anyplace else. In fact, you can't leave. We've frightened the children, each nest in turn, and told them of a gray wasteland, a ruined earth. I've said it so many times, it might even be true.

I have my comfortable room with its colorful rugs and weavings, its potted plants. Jake and I did get back together for a while when Tessa was growing up, but it didn't work any better that time than it had before. You know I met him when he was my math teacher at community college—when I was going for my nursing degree, before things changed. I used to tease him and say he was a problem I couldn't solve.

What was the problem? The sex would be great, then awkward. The conversation would be fun, then deadly boring. Then fun again. Jake once said we were anti-soulmates. We were destined to not be able to get along. Tessa linked us for a long time, and then the baby. It was a lot, but not enough.

We're friends now, but friends with the pressure of silence—a pact to not reveal each other's secrets, or perhaps even our own.

Tessa has been gone almost fifteen years. And I know she's still alive...but I won't allow that thought. I've told her daughter she is dead, and dead she must remain. That is all that is left to me, Tessa's daughter. Lithe, softhearted, with a wicked smile. The only child I ever truly gave to Golden. Sometimes I call her Tessa as if by mistake, but that isn't her real name.

Emi.

Emi, 2056

Emi could hear sobbing coming from the nest, or at least the part of the nest that was composed of heaps of quilts and blankets and some nooks for privacy. Sarah and Madden were breaking up again, and the heartbroken sobs were coming from Madden, of course. Sarah was always the one doing the breaking up.

When the sobbing changed to the heavy breathing and moaning of breakup sex, Emi moved out of range. Wrapped in a fleecy blanket, she sat by the cold hearth of the big room. And it was cold, with some snow softening the ground. But it was supposed to warm up later in the week.

"And how do the GUs KNOW that?" Matteo had demanded. GU was nest slang for grown-up. "How can anyone KNOW it is going to warm up?"

"I don't know how... look at the sky... the animals?"

"You think chickens know when it is going to warm up?"

She shook her head. "Matteo, chill out. Just relax. Ever since you found that... thing... you've been acting insane. Sure, maybe the GUs are lying to us, and why not, we're just kids."

"We were kids," he said. "Little kids. But I don't consider us children now. In a year, at seventeen, we'll be full members of Golden."

"We were little kids," she said. They looked at each other and smiled. That's when they'd fallen in love, aged two. They'd refused to be parted, had slept holding hands. If separated, Matteo wept, asking for my "one good friend." Emi went through a stage when she wouldn't eat unless he was eating the exact same thing. The GUs—his mom and her grandmother Maira, had been alternately charmed and annoyed.

"Maybe they'll grow up and get married," Maira had said, watching them.

"Well, I consider them engaged," Matteo's mom had said. But of course everyone had assumed that it was puppy love and that it was something they would grow out of.

They'd loved each other until they were twelve, then despised each other for two years, then figured out how to mutually lose their cumbersome virginities, then loved each other, hated each other, run off with other people and only recently settled back down to... love.

This last turn of events had not been greeted with enthusiasm by other people. The members of the Nest felt it was childish and that Emi and Matteo were going backwards instead of forwards into a more adult future. By that point Matteo wasn't close to his mother; he no longer cared about her opinion. But Maira was critical. Didn't Emi want to expand her experience? Look around more? Emi tried to explain but couldn't find the right words to deflect Maira.

One night when the criticism was too much, and Emi had walked off in the moonlight to sit on Pook's Hill, she'd made a vow, on the moon, on the dark, on stillness. She'd vowed to stop fighting with Matteo, at least about every little thing, and to always care for his welfare as much as for herself. She knew that usually these were things you vowed to the actual person, but she didn't want to freak Matteo out.

And now she was disagreeing with him again. "Matteo, what you saw doesn't prove anything. That thing could have been...anything. You didn't ask, no one else saw it."

"Fuck that," he said. "I didn't see 'a thing.' I saw, and heard, a shortwave radio, hidden in a shack way at the edge of the property. It was on, and I used it to talk to a man...a man a few hundred miles east of here, who said it was going to snow."

"It just sounds so...weird...so unlikely...are you sure?"

"I did not dream a shortwave radio. I'd seen the design in the Encyclopedia, so I understood it. And there was a manual, just open right next to it. Emi, they are lying. The world isn't destroyed. The whole world is right out there."

"Like down some dirt roads and then a paved highway? So close? I thought the world ended when we were toddlers. How can you believe there is a world?" Emi wanted to sound more sarcastic than it came out. Really, she just sounded curious.

"The signs have been there for a long time. Remember when we heard that noise in the sky and the GUs said it was thunder? But out of a cloudless sky? It must have been an airplane. But I'm guessing we're not on a big route or anything. That noise is occasional. I might have believed thunder when I was very little. But I look up, and a few times I know I've seen planes. Everyone else just isn't looking. It is obvious. Obvious! And you know you want to go, find out, you want to go with me."

Of course she did. "But what about my grandparents, especially my grandma? I'm all she's got. My mom left me...us...Golden...when I was a baby."

"I know," he said sympathetically.

"My mom died fighting the tyrants. That sounds, well, very brave to me. But my grandma hates her for leaving, for taking the risk. You know, sometimes she calls me Tessa, my mom's name, and I don't think it is by mistake. Like she is trying to keep my mom alive or secretly thinks maybe Tessa is alive."

"Maybe she is alive?" A soft voice, not Matteo's, asked.

"Who? My mom? Fuck you." Emi spun round. Co was crouched near them: long, tall, and skinny, cropped hair, sweet-faced. Normally Emi felt a rush of affection whenever she saw Co. But not now. "Are you eavesdropping?"

"I was trying to give you hope." Co said. "And besides, you were talking pretty loudly."

"Hope? For a person who is either just plain dead or who hasn't cared enough to try and see me in fifteen years?"

"Do you remember her?" Matteo asked.

"No. How could I? The story is, I was learning to walk, I took my first steps. And then she left."

"You know, she could be alive," Co said pensively.

"Stop saying that."

"Well, it's true. You have no proof that she's dead. I once heard my dad talking about her in the present tense and as if she were. Alive, that is."

"And the GUs have lied about everything," Matteo said, pressing his point.

"You are just trying to get me to leave with you," Emi said.

"Yes. Yes I am," he said.

"You're leaving? I want to go, too. Are you really serious? Matteo, I want to go," Co said. "I can't take it anymore. No one knows who I am. Everyone wants me to be… different… something… else. Something fixed. Something they can put in a box. And Liam is chasing my ass."

"Liam isn't all bad," Matteo said.

"No, but he's an idiot. He thinks I'm a girl, or he thinks he thinks that… why can't he leave me alone? Why doesn't anyone believe me? Why do I have to be one thing or the other?"

"I believe you," said Emi patting her friend's hand. "Would you really leave? If you leave, I think I will too. Without you and Matteo, what's left for me here? Although I'd miss Madden a lot."

"What about the rest of the nest?" Co asked.

"I'm going to ask them." Matteo said. "I've called a meeting. Tonight. Outside, on Pook's Hill."

"Cold," Emi shivered.

"We'll have a big bonfire. Bring your sleeping bags."

"Kind of dramatic way to have a meeting," she said.

He grinned. "Emi, you know me. Yes, it is dramatic. On purpose. I'm going to tell everyone we're leaving. And invite them to come."

"We," she said. He took her hand and squeezed it. "Matteo, how can you be so sure?"

"I'm not sure," he said. "But I'm ready to find out. To have an adventure. A quest. And I'm glad you are coming with me."

"So am I," Emi said.

They both looked at Co. "Thank God you want to come," Matteo said. "You're so smart about people, about everything. You know, you'd make a good leader, for the trip."

"OK," Co said, after hesitating only an instant. That

was very like Co—insecure one minute, definitive the next.

Emi just smiled—a smile of relief, of fear, and of the unexpected.

The sound of Madden sobbing again reached them across the big, cold room. They got up and stretched and went their separate ways.

Matteo could have predicted it, if he hadn't been so wrapped up in his own excitement. The meeting on Pook's Hill was not going well, at least from his point of view.

"Who cares that the GUs are lying to us? Adults always lie to children. I'll lie to my own someday." Akira shook back his blond mane of hair and sucked smoke out of the pipe in his mouth. Sarah looked at him adoringly. They were a brand new couple.

Madden shrank back from the heat of the bonfire into the shadows of the dancing flames.

Co moved in to rescue Matteo. Co said, "It doesn't matter if it is good or bad, if they lied to protect us or to control us. They lied. That may have been their prerogative, but it is over now. So we're going."

"To seek your fortunes?" Sarah asked sarcastically.

"And my mother might be alive," Emi said. Then wished she hadn't said anything. In any case, everyone ignored the topic.

"You're just...going?" Liam asked. "Like camping? Just taking your packs and bedrolls?"

"Yes," said Co. "And we know we can trust you not to tell." Everyone nodded their heads. They might disagree, but they were still the nest.

"But what about...training, apprenticeships. Matteo, weren't you learning about fuels, ethanol, the solar panels? Emi, weren't you going to be a midwife with your grandmother?" Akira asked.

"We're going," said Co.

"Who is we?" said Liam.

"Me, Matteo, and Emi, and...." Co scanned the group. Sparks flew upward, illuminating the humped turtle shape of the small mountain behind them.

"You're taking the tunnel?" Liam continued.

Matteo nodded. "Of course. Remember years ago when we found the tunnel in that old abandoned mine? And shored it up, but it was pretty safe, pretty clean. Well, I think now that the GUs were maintaining it. Using it to get in and out of Golden. That's why we never run out of things—antibiotics, salt, condoms. The world is still there. And the GUs are still going back and forth."

"Fuck," said Liam. "Sounds true."

"It is true," Matteo was scratching the dirt with a stick.

"So who is going—Matteo, Co, Emi." Liam's eyes were on Co.

"And me," Madden said with a half sob. "Because Sarah, you don't care, maybe you never cared, and my heart is broken, and you don't even notice." She wiped her eyes. "I'm going."

"Half the nest!" said Liam. "Just like that."

"More than half," Matteo corrected him in that precise way of his that drove Emi insane. Still, she squeezed his hand.

Liam's eyes were hot on Co. But Co glared at him, with a hatred that was hard to ignore. Still, Liam kept talking. "Won't you miss Golden? Here you know everyone, and there is no violence, and it's beautiful. Maybe the GUs are lying, and the world really is still there. But is the world a good place? We were born here. Our parents chose this. I like it here. Won't you be homesick out there where people don't know you?"

His remarks were met with silence from Matteo and the rest.

"Well," said Akira, standing up and shaking himself off. "Sarah. Liam. It looks like we're the only loyal ones. It looks like we're the ones who are going to have to stay and protect Golden. To take care of the future. To not abandon our ideals." The three of them grouped together, then turned and walked away. They did not say good-bye.

Matteo was fuming that his truth had not caught fire with everyone. Co was smiling, a grin of relief that Liam had left. Emi heard a small voice in her head, cheery, and slightly stunned with surprise, that said: "well, we're off."

Madden blew her nose. "Huh," she said. "That wasn't so hard. You know, I feel better. Let's get organized. Let's start packing. Let's go."

They left before dawn. The pale red light would be beautiful in the hills, but they were no longer there to see it.

Emi had gone to see Maira the night before, after the bonfire. Not exactly to say good-bye, but to say… something. Perhaps to double-check her feelings. But the room was empty. Maira wasn't there. Emi couldn't quite imagine where she'd gone. Maira had a few occasional lovers, but gone for the whole night? It was late, and the room was dark, the bed neatly made. Emi sat for a moment, smelling Maira, the lavender and peppery sweat of her grandmother's droopy breasts and soft arms. Maira had been her mother—cosseted her, protected her, stood up for her, nurtured her—as much as Golden allowed for one person to be a mother. Regret at leaving, at hurting Maira, swept over Emi. She wasn't going to be able to leave. It was just too harsh. She was going to have to tell Matteo she was staying behind.

But Maira's things, without Maira, proved irresistible. An overstuffed drawer, a box with a lock that also sported a tiny key, an untidy underwear drawer all called to her. It had always been Emi's habit to riffle through Maira's things, and when Emi was little, Maira had let her try on the earrings, arrange the buttons and coins, gently touch a few treasures.

Rummaging through a pile of scarves, a large dirty envelope came to hand. It had paper money in it—Emi vaguely knew what that was—ten bills showing the number one hundred and six bills showing twenty. Money? Would that be useful? Emi kept browsing underpants, finding a surprisingly small pair of black lace ones. There was also a lovely pair of long silver earrings, filigree, set with some kind of small, sparkly blue stones.

And then something unusual came to hand. A small stack of letters and cards, tied with a string. And, to her surprise, addressed to her, Emi.

They'd been opened, and by the look, were already pretty old. A yellowed envelope revealed a cheerful card with smiling animals and HAPPY BIRTHDAY EMI! written in bold, slightly slanting handwriting. It had been sent from Albuquerque, New Mexico, when Emi was four. That was printed right on the envelope. It was signed in the same handwriting. LOVE, MOMMY.

Emi felt as if she was going to faint, to vomit, or

both. There was a long letter written on lined paper to Maira. It began: "Dear Maira, what the fuck is wrong with you? What the fuck?"

Emi was trembling so violently the paper shook. Her mind had ceased to function, but not her hands. She took the little stack of letters and went back to the envelope of money and took it. She hesitated, then added the earrings too. She put everything in her backpack and turned and bolted out of Maira's room, not closing the door behind her.

She thought about seeing her grandfather, Jake. But why? He'd been lying to her too. And she was leaving and sworn not to tell anyone. Yet somehow, she thought, he of all people might understand. After all, he was different himself. He was a black man and mostly everyone else at Golden was white or a mix of things. She looked like him, although he'd laugh and say he'd never be pretty like she was. Also, he walked with a limp, a cane. He was strong but tired easily. When she was little she'd asked him what had happened to his leg, and he'd said an angel had wrecked it in a wrestling match.

But of course that couldn't be true. And she didn't go to find him now.

Back at the nest she finished packing, smoked two hits, and curled herself into a ball, sobbed for a few minutes, and slept for a few hours. Even in her sleep she seemed to be thinking about Tessa. Her mother. She didn't understand exactly where the letters had been sent from, but she'd figure it out. Matteo could help her.

In the dead of night, Matteo came and got her. It would be hours until the sun rose over the eastern rim of the Commune of the Golden Sun. Its rays touched the central area with the kitchen and dining room.

Soon children would appear, running about and swinging from the climbing structure. Coffee would be set out for early risers.

It would not be long before Golden realized another four of its children were gone.

They left in a line, Co first. Then Emi, as if she had some idea of where they were going. Then Madden, with her huge pack. Then Matteo at the end, herding them. This had been his habit since he was little, keeping everyone together. Emi called him *the sheepdog*. Co's lanky silhouette was outlined against the starry sky. Emi looked at Co's back, a back she had known since babyhood, a back she had chased in tag and looked for in hide and seek.

The shape of each person was as familiar to Emi as her own hands or feet. Except that she'd never seen Co naked. None of them had. Co always kept on an old, loose pair of bathing trunks. Even sleeping.

No moon, but they knew the first part of the path well. Through the old mine, keeping mostly to the right to avoid any standing water. Ten minutes or so through the tunnel, shored up with beams to replace any rotting timbers.

And then the tunnel emerged into scrub, juniper and piñon. "We're going north," Madden said behind Emi. "North and east."

"Why?"

"Matteo and Co say there should be some small towns there, along the train tracks."

"And why are we going to a small town?"

"We have to start somewhere. Matteo says that there is a big city to the north."

"Matteo says, Matteo says…." Emi grumbled. "And

why north?"

"Because of the map."

"What map?"

"This map," Madden waved a children's book at her. It had frayed cardboard covers and a crude map on the front. The title: Asi Es Nuevo Mexico: This Is New Mexico. And there on the map was the name Albuquerque. However, Emi had her doubts.

"New Mexico isn't a place anymore," she said.

"We don't know that," Co said from the front. "If the world is still there, why not New Mexico? And people. And trains running along the tracks." They'd all seen the remains of tracks, corroding in the weeds. And a rickety trestle and abandoned freight cars sitting out on the earth. Golden even had a few for storage.

They'd all been camping, sometimes alone and sometimes with each other, for as long as they could remember. They were allowed to go west and south, but never more than a two day's walk in either direction. Otherwise the boundaries were clear...a huge dead oak tree, an abandoned stock pond. And a juncture of train tracks marked the western and southern limit. Of course they'd crossed the tracks, feeling bold. But never ventured more than a few steps into the forbidden terrain.

Emi almost stumbled. She knew what trains were from picture books. There was a heap of children's books, easy to read, in the neglected outbuilding called the library at Golden. The way the world was, had been, when there was a world. Not censored, not discussed, and not usually read. Like this New Mexico book with the childishly drawn map. Jake had read some things to her the same way he'd taught her a bit of history and algebra. He'd been a teacher, after all. But she didn't really have a whole picture of much of anything outside of Golden.

They walked along now in silence. The sun had risen, and it was getting warmer. Cactus wrens twittered by, and thrashers called. A rabbit scooted across the arroyo in front of them. They were in the dry watercourse now. Madden kept her eyes down, looking for fossils and pretty or unusual pebbles.

"Fuck," said Co. "In all that rush to leave, I forgot to take enough water."

"I've got purification tablets," said Madden. "Plus extra rope, bandages, and some cookies."

Co and Emi laughed. "It's good you came along, Maddy," Co said, "even if you are all weepy and heartbroken about someone who doesn't deserve you."

Madden was happy to be called by her nickname. She thought about what Co had said about Sarah. It was a nice thing to say, but it wasn't true. Sarah was more beautiful, cooler, more self-assured. She was even taller. Madden had been the lucky one; at least she'd thought so at the start. Now she was unlucky. Alone, without Sarah.

They camped for lunch on a flat stone. Uphill a ways there was a small stream, and they purified some water. The world had been poisoned, and this was one of the results. Cow patties baked in the sun.

"I knew it," Matteo said. "Cow shit. Look at it!"

"So what?" said Emi.

"COWS," Matteo pronounced. "And whose cows? People are running cattle out here."

"Maybe from Golden?" she ventured.

The three of them looked at her, all shaking their heads.

"No way," said Madden. "Way too far. And I know our cows, they'd never be here."

"People," said Co. "Other people."

Matteo gave a wide grin. "I knew it, I knew it, I knew it!"

"Yes," said Co. "And we knew you were right. Come on. Time to keep going."

Tessa, 2041-2056

Tessa argued with her mother, Maira, every day. Usually when she was driving to work. Although Tessa hadn't seen her mother in fifteen years, although Tessa had left and never returned, it was as if Maira was in the passenger seat, criticizing her.

"You couldn't bicycle to work? This is your idea of an ecological choice?" the imaginary Maira said.

Tessa could have said—"Shut the fuck up, you're a phantom." Or she could have mentioned the bicycle theft rate. Thieves just sawed through the locks in seconds. And how there was no place to park a bike in her already crowded office. But instead she went on a long, boring explanation of her electric car.

Tessa fiddled with the car sound system, made the music almost loud enough to drown her mother out. A particular song blared from the speakers. That song that always reminded her of how she'd left Golden.

The cadre of soldiers had picked up the Four out at an intersection of county roads along flat agricultural land.

Tessa had hopped into a van crammed full of people and packs. The driver, charcoal and grease paint streaks beneath her eyes, cranked up some music.

Tessa had never heard anything like it. She had heard very little canned music, which was increasingly banned at Golden. All they had was live drumming. And now every hair on her arm stood up. The nape of her neck tingled violently. *We Are The Champions* poured from the speakers.

Tessa was frozen. "Is this...a religion?" she whispered to the guy sitting next to her.

"Queen?" he laughed. "I guess you could say so."

Maybe a religion with a ruling queen? And her champions?

Years later, Tessa would have to smile at herself. And be grateful that she hadn't shared her imaginings. She still loved the song. That bit about *keep on fighting* always brought tears to her eyes.

"Turn it down," the phantom Maira said. "I can't believe you are listening to that old song. It has got to be a hundred years old."

"More like seventy-five," Tessa said.

Maira just sniffed.

Seen from the air, Tessa's life looked fine. Partner, job, and yes—electric car. True, this is not what she had been raised for. She'd spent her childhood wild, naked, roaming the countryside. That is when she had been little, and Maira had been large. And the arbiter of everything. Maira, warm and soft, always letting Tessa sleep, cozy, in the bed with her. Maira, sometimes silent, sometimes bossy, but always—there.

Albuquerque had its tall buildings, skyscrapers. It had shocked Tessa at first. The buildings at Golden were two-story at most. You could run up Pook's Hill and look down on the hamlet. And Albuquerque had problems too: violence, car theft, break-ins, junkies. Water was rationed to the point that there was a limit to how much you could buy at one time, how many jugs. It was just like cold medication, a limited purchase. But cold medication could be cooked into speed. Water was just for cooking. Not to mention everything else in life. But she wasn't going to mention problems like this to the invisible Maira, who would just say Golden was better.

How old had she been when she had understood that Maira was a person, a woman, too? Certainly not when she, Tessa, had split from Golden in a cloud of self-righteous, idealistic rage. She was sure the world was ending and that she was going to be a hero and a warrior.

What had been the look on Maira's face? Maira had turned away, cursing her. Tessa could see the Sandias, mountains both lumpy and beautiful. Was that Mount Taylor, far off to the west, but visible when there wasn't too much haze? She and Paulus should go hiking this weekend, maybe up to the Valles Caldera. You could see that volcanic crater from the moon.

Yes, some of the forests were dying, drying up from too many winters without snow. But it was still beautiful. They should just set all the house alarms and go. Take a break.

Tessa turned to see if Maira was still there, buckled into the passenger seat, but her mother was gone.

When Tessa had left Golden, it was for good. But she hadn't given that any thought at the time. She had just gone, along with the rest of the Four. The war was raging, civil war against a tyrant who refused to step down from power despite the outcome of the elections. Cities were in flames. Masked protestors threw molotov cocktails and in turn were gunned down. Golden had been full of refugees. Friends of friends arrived; people who had lived there twenty years ago for a month appeared, children in tow. The buildings were bursting. Sleeping bags were everywhere. Cooks grumbled and food managers scrimped.

Then Golden closed its doors. Maira had been a supporter of this plan. Jake had opposed it. However, people called him a romantic and even accused him of not caring about Golden as it was. Eventually he gave in and consensus was reached. Civil war continued for years. In those days, however, there was still some news of the outside world.

Tessa's actual nest was small—the Four. Four girls, now women, they'd been together since childhood. Tessa had given birth to Emi just when the turmoil was starting to get worse. If she knew who the father was, she didn't say. And no one cared, or at least no one expressed curiosity in the face of Tessa's impassivity. She nursed the baby, weaned her at a year, and put her in Maira's arms. Then the Four departed, to fight in the final battles. And fight they did, on the streets of Albuquerque, as part of a human chain across I-25.

More than a decade later Tessa's husband Paulus still enjoyed her stories. "Is this the intersection you blew up?" he'd ask at the I-40 interchange. Of course the answer was yes. He'd spent the war in prison. He'd been captured at the start and spent the remainder starving in a camp in the Manzanos. The impact was still there. He was still lanky, a little too thin even approaching early middle age.

After the Four left Golden, the commune sealed itself off more securely from the outside. Soon the GUs started telling the children there was no outside world. It had been destroyed. All that was left was a desolate wasteland. And only a self-destructive fool would want to see what was out there.

Tessa had been ill-prepared for war. She had not even been so much as hit as a child. Golden forbade it, and Maira wasn't prone to it. Boys didn't grab girls and pull down their underpants. People didn't even call each other bad names. She could shoot of course.

Everyone at Golden could. And she could clean a gun, store it, and handle a rifle as well as a handgun. For Golden, it was just part of ranching, of living in the country.

She and the Four and a group of cadres had been handed weapons and supplies. They'd been dropped off at one of the library buildings at the University of New Mexico campus and instructed to hold the building and the plaza in front of it. This worked for several weeks, and food was resupplied.

Then the government forces had turned east and swept through them, leaving corpses. Two of the Four were blown to bits, right next to each other. Crystal and Tessa hadn't even been able to identify them, although of course they knew who they were.

Crystal had slashed her wrists that night, and Tessa had bandaged and nursed her through. It gave them both something to do. Tessa didn't think about killing herself then, as she was planning—in some vague, unspecified way—to go back to Emi. Crystal got better, but slowly, and Tessa certainly couldn't leave her. They got moved out to other locations, and ended up part of the huge human chain and barricade that blocked I-25 once and for all.

The barricade had been amazing. Tens of thousands of people—at one time it was claimed half a million, but that sounded exaggerated to Tessa—camped out on the interstate. They had barricades of lawn furniture, old appliances, cars, and more.

People slept in tents, cooked on camping stoves. There were porta-potties and latrine trenches. For three months they shut down Interstate traffic in New Mexico. Tessa remembered singing and guitars. At least two babies were born there, and a few people died of natural causes. The night two food trucks appeared in the quadrant where Tessa was living had been exciting. One served tacos and one pan-Asian noodles. They were giving the food away for free. Tessa stood on line for hours, first for noodles, then for tacos. It was worth it.

This was at the end of the war. Almost ninety percent of the population was fighting the Tyrant's army and police. Many of those forces hated the Tyrant too, and starting going over to the so-called rebels. The rebels who had just wanted the Tyrant to concede when he'd lost his last election.

The war ended. Tessa washed the war paint off her cheeks for the last time. They'd worn camouflage: smears of black and brown and green on their faces. There was no reason; it was just a fad. Everyone in the cities did. After that, Tessa couldn't wear so much as lipstick. You still saw it around though, after the war: people with just a patch of camouflage on a cheek, showing the status of a veteran.

Crystal recovered, married a nice woman, bought a house in the North Valley, kept chickens, and raised two children. She sold at the Growers' Market and made beaded jewelry. Her life was like a little piece of Golden, only with more shopping and no rules. Her car had been stolen twice: once recovered, then trashed. But that was just the price of living in the city.

She and Tessa saw each other once a week for coffee and talked about this and that, never anything serious or requiring much response. But neither of them ever missed a date.

When she left to go fight, Tessa hadn't given a thought to what Golden might do— she figured she'd be a victor, or dead, in six months. If dead, she'd still have done the best for her child's future. If alive, she'd come right back.

It had taken more than a year to win the war. That last year had been the bloodiest.

Tessa had written Maira every chance she had but never heard back. She knew someone must still be still going out as a town tripper, but there was no response from her mother. Then the war ended.

The city was full of traumatized veterans. They wanted to be together and although there were endless support groups and 12-step meetings and mental health clinics most vets gravitated towards the bars and parties. One church opened up to vets from Friday evening through early Monday morning. You could spend the whole weekend mingling and camping out in the church's social hall, eating, crying, praying, arguing, and flirting. That's where Tessa met Paulus.

"Are you ok?," he'd asked her. "You look worried."

"This is just how I look."

"Want to go outside and smoke?"

"No thanks."

"There's contact improv in the basement."

Tessa laughed. "Not my thing."

"What would you like to do?" he asked.

"Meaningless making out might help me."

"Does it have to be totally meaningless?"

"Absolutely," she said as she drew close and started kissing him passionately.

Then they went to bed together at Tessa's apartment, and fell in love. Tessa went to nursing school, wrote Emi once a month, sent a birthday card, then another. But she still heard nothing back.

Years began to pass, each one more quickly.

"We'll go get her," said Paulus.

"Maira won't let me see her. Golden won't let us in."

"Tessa, you were a soldier. You mean you can't go visit your own child?"

"It might be too disruptive. She won't know me. Besides, the whole thing will upset Maira. What if Emi wants to go with me? It would break Maira's heart."

"Which is it? She won't know you or she'll want you?"

"Paulus, I don't ask you about your toes. Don't ask me any more about this."

He'd lost his two smallest toes on his left foot in the camps and refused to say a word about it. They both had secrets, and usually it worked.

"I respect your privacy, Tessa," he said. "But still, don't you think...?"

"No," she said. "No, I don't."

"Then let's have a child," he said. "Or two. We're still young enough. You know I come from a big family and I always wanted kids."

"No," said Tessa.

"It's nice here," he gestured to the patio, the potted plants, the mourning doves cooing in the trees. "We've got enough room, we could make it work."

"There's not enough rain. There's too much crime," she said and shook her head. Like the song, she'd fight to the end—even if the end of fighting was already here.

And she was too stupid, or too stubborn, to see it. Had something inside her died along with two of the Four? With the loss of Emi? She couldn't ask Paulus if she'd changed, because he hadn't known her before. She couldn't ask Crystal, because Crystal was incapable of talking about the past.

Of course she was different. After all, nothing stayed the same. Albuquerque was changing. Many of the big cottonwoods in the bosque had died off. The beautiful flocks of sandhill cranes that migrated across the sky above the city were smaller. There were fewer of the majestic birds, but they still wintered in local fields.

In contrast, the city itself was livelier than when she'd first settled there. There was an endless array of delicious restaurants: Greek, Thai, sushi joints, noodle places. And some things didn't change. You could come out of a restaurant and find your car gone. You could get knocked over and mugged in broad daylight. And Tessa's clinic was still full of old ladies with diabetes who worried about affording enough medication every month.

Sometimes Tessa had a fantasy that in some way a version of herself was still at Golden. Maybe her double was still there, a woman who looked just like her. Who had never left but stayed home. Maybe this woman was happy as Emi's mother, enjoying watching her grow up. A woman who was at peace with Maira, her own mother, who in this fantasy was pleasant and kind.

But Tessa couldn't really keep this version alive, even if just in her imagination. Because, if she was honest, when she saw herself at Golden, she couldn't enjoy it, because she was in some kind of coma. Sleeping. Completely unconscious.

Emi, 2056

By the third night out, Emi missed being alone with Matteo. They'd been sleeping in a group around the fire, the way they usually did when out camping from Golden.

Madden was a fire master. She'd get a blaze going with just one match and wake faithfully in the night to bank the coals for morning coffee.

Emi sent Matteo a series of meaningful glances throughout the day. That was all that was needed to rendezvous a bit after supper. In a private spot, they zipped their sleeping bags together and made love with silent, practiced passion. They were used to keeping quiet and not disturbing others. Besides, Matteo had a shy streak and Emi would never embarrass him. Instead of yelling, she ran her fingernails hard along his back and gasped for his ears only.

Afterwards, Emi put her head on Matteo's shoulder. His fingers drummed out a rhythm on her arm. He pointed out the constellations. Far to the north there was a dim glow on the horizon.

"Albuquerque...." he said.

"Are you sure? I think my mom's there." Emi had told him about the letters from Tessa to Maira, but wouldn't let him see them. That would be too real, and all the hate and confusion she felt might come to the surface and she'd start flipping out.

"I'm sure."

"We should go. I want to find her. I just want that so much. I was glad to leave Golden but now I want something more. My mom."

"We're heading in that direction," Matteo said. "I see no reason we won't eventually get there.

"A city big enough to light up the sky," Emi murmured and fell asleep.

The next morning their path went down in altitude. It was sunny, a little warmer.

A bull snake slithered by, and Madden got ready to catch it until Matteo, still behind her, said "Maddy! No snakes!" and everyone laughed.

It was now the fourth day out from Golden. Of course they'd been out camping before, sometimes for days, but only in the approved directions. And with every intention of coming back.

Co seemed taller, making small decisions with authority. Madden really had come well-prepared, producing lentils, socks, and her homemade lip balm at the needed moments. She found wild cress growing in a stream and harvested piñon nuts that had survived the winter without being eaten by a variety of small animals. It seemed as if she could go on like this forever.

Matteo was happy—happier than Emi had ever seen him. At Golden, he'd been a happy child. But later his mom had had more kids with a different dad, and Matteo had fallen into his own world. And Emi understood now that he'd been looking—looking for proof of lies. That was not a happy spot.

She snuck a look at him, back at the end of the line. Medium height, skinny, soft brown skin and a mop of dark hair. "Random," she'd teased him. "Your hair is just... random." Sometimes it stuck straight up, making him looked alarmed, or like someone who had lost a hairbrush.

He was dressed in the odd, mismatched things he

favored out of Golden's clothing warehouse—a pair of madras pants and a striped shirt. Emi squinted... was he cute?

Sometimes people said that she and he looked alike. To her chagrin, when they were having their polyamorous year (and a half), other people did think Matteo was cute.

He'd looked really handsome then, when she didn't possess him. At least, thank goodness, his lovers had been from the older nest. There were strict rules at Golden forbidding adults from messing around with teenagers, at least until the teenagers were full members. But there were still plenty of options with people a little older or a little younger. As if by mutual agreement, both she and Matteo had kept off of their own nest during that time of walkabout. And she'd had opportunities, plenty, she reminded herself reassuringly. Probably more than Matteo. "It's easier for girls," he'd said, but she didn't agree. Maybe she was slightly cuter than Matteo? Or less preoccupied?

What did she, Emi, look like? It was hard to tell about yourself. Curly hair. Nice medium-sized breasts. Smaller breasts than Madden's, but bigger than Sarah's. But this kind of thing wasn't going to matter anymore, she realized with a kind of shock. If they met people, those people wouldn't know Sarah's breast size or Matteo's old lovers or what childhood was like in Golden—muddy, sunburned, happy to hear the dinner bell ring.

And then, coming over a crest, Emi saw the ruined city.

Madden was just going along, hour by hour. When the sun went behind a cloud, her heart started to ache for Sarah. Sarah had been the first, the only... well, what? Lover? Beloved? She'd felt Sarah was perfection itself, but maybe that was just her imagination. After all, Emi had never really liked Sarah. And Co, who was generally kind and accepting, went silent when Madden praised Sarah.

Still, her other friends couldn't know how lonely Madden was. She usually just shrugged her situation off to them. After all, her mom had died a long time ago. She'd never known her dad, and when her mom got sick, Golden cared for Madden and her mom. And when her mom had died, all the other moms had taken Madden in and cared for her.

Someone had once told her that in the outside world, before it ended, kids who had no parents were sent to something called foster care, where they could be hurt or abused. Of course that didn't happen at Golden.

Co was keeping a steady pace. Maybe a bit too fast for Emi and a bit too slow for Matteo, but it was working. Everyone seemed fine. They passed through an upland with beautiful red rocks carved by the wind and then into a bit of a slot canyon.

Maybe that was why it was so hard to let go of Sarah. Being with Sarah had been special. For the first time since her mom had died, Madden had been someone's one and only. But then she really wasn't that, not in any true way.

Her heart constricted again. Could this kind of pain kill you? It felt like it could. Was a heartbreak like a heart attack? It hurt so much. Madden had never imagined that anything could hurt like this. She'd tried to explain it to Emi, but Emi had just gone off on her ridiculous rant about how Matteo had run around on her during that year they took off from each other. Who cared? They were back together now, two peas in a pod. Madden tried to feel jealous, but she couldn't really.

She was happy they were happy.

A cluster of turkey vultures rode the thermals above them. When they were kids, people said turkey vultures were gross because they ate dead things. But Madden liked them. The world would be horrible if no one cleaned up. And she knew what it was like to scour the land for anything edible.

Still following Co's lead, they crested a small hill. Down below, there was something that looked like a city.

Walls of red adobe brick rose imposingly. It had once been a large building, enclosed in a series of walls, with courtyards and smaller rooms.

"Maybe the world has ended?" Madden said. "And this was a town that got destroyed?"

The four of them had come to a halt and as one had dropped their packs and themselves to the ground. The walls reflected the warmth of the late afternoon sun. A golden light filled the space, but soon enough darkness would fall, still early around the spring equinox.

"No, I think it is old," said Matteo.

"Old old?" asked Madden. "Like the village under Pook's Hill?"

"I'm guessing," he said.

"I think so, too," said Co, and held up a large, broken piece of pottery. Red and black lines zig-zagged boldly across the shard. It looked like the pieces they found everywhere in the land around Golden.

No one on the commune paid much attention to history, but Matteo knew a little.

Jake liked to talk about it. "A thousand years old, maybe. Remember how Jake used to read to us from that pamphlet about the land around us? This is from when people lived off corn and squash and beans. And fishing and hunting."

"Like Golden," Madden said.

"Well, we have cows," said Co. "I mean, we had cows....Anyway, there are cows at Golden."

They all fell silent for a moment. "I like it here," Co continued. "Can we camp? It's a little early to stop, but we all could use a bit of a rest."

Everyone nodded. They picked a spacious, roofless room, the floor hard-packed and scoured by sun and wind. It made a cozy spot, with sleeping bags and campfire.

It did feel familiar to Emi. Her grandfather had liked to talk about the people who had lived here before. These were the people who had built cities before the Spanish came. Once he had tried to get a bunch of kids to build a model of these pueblos out of tiny adobe bricks. But the children of Golden soon lost interest in any school-type project and the unfinished building was left dry and cracked on a windowsill. Still, Emi was glad she knew a little about all this. If she hadn't, the ruin might have frightened her.

Co and Matteo were conferring. They seemed pleased—the supplies were holding up. The sun went down, and they ate a thick soup.

Emi got up to pee, came back, and saw two new and unfamiliar figures sitting by the fire.

"Oh hello...oh, excuse me," she half stuttered with surprise.

She'd only been gone a minute, and yet here were two visitors chatting away with her friends, as if they had been there for hours.

"Emi," Co said. "This is Pine and Willow. They were passing through, and, you know... it's late. So we gave them some soup and invited them to camp for the night."

It was odd to meet strangers. At Golden, there were none and no introductions, no partings.

The old couple, sitting cross-legged on the earth, seemed nice enough to Emi. Both had faces that disappeared in creases and wrinkles. They both had long white hair and tattered, grayish robes and looked older, a lot older, than anyone Emi had ever seen.

"Evening," the old woman said. "The soup is delicious. I hear you had a hand in making it."

Emi nodded.

She felt comfortable and uncomfortable at the same time.

The evening passed peacefully. The old couple seemed to have heard of Golden and didn't ask any awkward or prying questions. They confirmed that the town of Mountainview was to the east, maybe two days' walk. And Albuquerque was indeed north of that.

"But there is a place you might like to visit that is closer," the old man said. He took a stick and drew a rough map in the dirt—east, a bit south. "Hardly out of your way," he continued. "There's music, big concerts that go on for days. It's called Blue Arrow. And there is another part... but well, you should go and see for yourselves."

Co perked up at the suggestion of music. Co was a good drummer, but there was no other kind of music at Golden. Sometimes one of the GUs would sing but then quickly fall silent if anyone was listening.

Matteo was following the map closely. Then he'd be able to hold it in his mind. He could get them to Blue Arrow, if they wanted to go.

Madden shifted uneasily, as if she didn't trust the strangers. But it wasn't as if they had any particular plan. They were just walking, walking away from Golden.

Everyone went to bed, but Emi couldn't sleep. She'd been afraid to read the letters from her mother, but now she really wanted to. She walked off a bit by herself and opened the packet with a gentle rustle, then turned on her flashlight.

But she couldn't start. Her throat constricted, her heart pounded, tears blurred her eyes. Her hands started shaking.

"Mija," Emi heard the old woman's voice. The old woman touched her cheek as gently as a falling leaf might. "Child. Shall I keep you company? It is a good time to read those letters, although I know it is hard."

Did she know what was in the letters? It seemed unlikely. But her voice was so soothing that Emi instantly felt comforted.

"You'll stay with me? Should I read them to you?" Emi asked.

"Or to yourself. I'll stay."

Emi followed the circle of light, reading. It was basically the same letter over and over, from her mother Tessa. *"I love the child. Please let me see Emi. Kiss her for me. Can I come back to visit? Or you could meet me outside Golden...anywhere. I'm fine, I'm married, I have a house. Can I see her? Please let me. I'm a nurse, mom, taking care of people just like you do. Can I see her?"*

Emi stopped shaking. She could feel the warmth of the old woman's body behind her, calming her.

"My mother wanted me. She didn't come back, but she wanted to," Emi said.

"Then she still wants you. Mothers do that, you know."

"She might be findable. That's really why I'm on this trip. Of course I wanted to go with Matteo, but my mom is my real reason. If I just showed up, would it work?"

"Where is she?"

"I think she is in Albuquerque."

"Not that far, really. It's a big place, but not that big. And I bet she's waiting, even if she doesn't realize yet that you are coming. Go find her. It's for the best."

"But to Blue Arrow first?"

"Blue Arrow is good. This journey is good."

"OK. I believe you."

"And I believe in you, mija." A soft sound, a gentle cough, and the old woman retreated. Then, as if she'd forgotten something, she came back to Emi's side.

"Maybe you should write her, your mother."

"You mean, like now? Tell her I'm coming?"

"Um hmm." The old woman nodded and turned again to go.

Once she was gone, Emi mulled over the idea. It wasn't hard, as she had paper and pencil in her pack. Then she wrote.

Dear Mom,

this is Emi. I always thought you were dead, that's why I didn't write before. And Maira never gave me anything you sent, not the cards or anything. I'm really sorry about that. Maira can be a bitch. (Emi then went and crossed that sentence out. It didn't seem right.) *Anyway, now I know you are alive. At least I'm pretty sure you are. You must be. I miss you a lot. I guess I always have. But I'm fine. Matteo and I and some friends have left Golden and are walking to Albuquerque. You don't know Matteo yet, but you'll meet him. He's my boyfriend and he is a wonderful person. So, we're coming to find you. I'm sure that we will.*

love, Emi

Emi looked at the letter, and reread the dim words by firelight. She was glad she'd written it, but of course, come to think, had no way to send it. She had no address for Tessa. She didn't even know how to mail a letter. Didn't you need a stamp or something?

She paused, then crumpled it up and tossed it into the flames.

Surely it might reach Tessa that way, through the sparks that flew up into the sky.

Then Emi went to bed, putting the letters from Tessa back into her pack.

In the morning, the old couple were gone from their spot, leaving just the four of them. Against a warm red wall a pretty willow tree seemed to be thriving on snowmelt and rain off a shattered roof.

"They got up early and left." Matteo said. "But we got some cool advice. Let's go to Blue Arrow."

Madden was packing up but looking worried.

"Do you think this Blue Arrow is safe? I mean, what if it isn't?"

"Things aren't safe, Maddy," Matteo said. "Relax. This is our adventure. I wonder where those old folks went."

Co and Emi smiled at each other. Co's eyes went to the tree as did Emi's. It was probably just a sweet coincidence, Emi thought. It wasn't that the old lady was actually a tree spirit, but rather that sometimes things were like each other and were drawn together. Maybe that is why she, Emi, was being drawn towards her mother.

The world was wide and could be quite mysterious. She'd felt that even as a child at Golden, particularly when rain fell suddenly, and double rainbows appeared in the sky. And now, no longer at Golden, she felt it even more.

Plus, it made her happy to notice something that Matteo had failed to see. It was true that Matteo knew a lot, but he didn't know everything. If the old lady really had turned back into a willow, Matteo was too preoccupied to see it.

Back out on their trail, across scrub and anthills and arroyos, there was a tinge of new excitement in the travelers. In the distance there were mountains still covered in light snow, and the sky rose above everything, a peerless blue. Almost the same color, a flock of bluebirds rustled in dry grass, then took off in a lovely arc. Madden saw a tarantula, an unusual blond one, and went towards its hairy body with her quick hand.

She touched it lightly, then withdrew. There was no way her human companions would put up with such an addition. Madden felt happy, though. Increasingly she had to remind herself to mope over Sarah. She didn't want to cheer up too fast and forget the love of her life.

It was the first time that they were going towards something, rather than just away.

Matteo had been so determined to leave Golden that he hadn't realized at first how lucky he was not to be alone. Of course he'd wanted Emi. But Co and even Madden were a great advantage. Madden's pack was an endless supply of necessities. Co led lightly and surely. When Emi and Matteo bickered, Co said, "Now children, do I have to separate you?" and made them laugh.

Co felt good about heading to this Blue Arrow place, whatever it was. Co had been desperate to leave Golden, too, but hadn't realized it, hadn't even known it was a possibility. But as soon as Matteo had mentioned it, Co wanted in… or rather, out. Co had always liked being outdoors and camping, because it wasn't about other people. But the three people following Co were not a problem. Emi and Madden sometimes seemed similar, in that they were led by their hearts. And both of them were broken-hearted, although Emi didn't seem to know it yet. Losing her mother was worse than Madden losing Sarah, who really was not a nice person in any case. Madden was much better off without Sarah in the long run, but the same could not be said of Emi without Tessa.

Co hadn't given much thought to Co's own parents, abruptly left behind without explanation or a goodbye. Co had left a note but no more than that. They'd probably be very hurt. They were sweet people, still a couple, but clueless when it came to Co. Like everyone else, they wanted something from Co that Co could not provide. A label. A box. An ordinary clarity.

"But I don't have to give anybody anything right now," Co thought, bursting into a cheerful whistle. There was supposed to be music: actual, real music at Blue Arrow. What would that be like?

Matteo had the map in his head and every so often gave a bit of direction to Co and the group. He hadn't imagined anything beyond leaving. This journey was known in some ways—the landscape, the people—and yet utterly new.

The old couple had been nice. He'd enjoyed meeting people he hadn't known his whole life, although they'd been oddly familiar. Things were going well. He'd had a hole in his sock that was creating the start of a blister, and Madden had darned it. She seemed like she was finally getting over Sarah. If he never heard about Sarah again, it would be too soon.

But what about Emi? Everyone else was jolly, and she seemed more preoccupied than usual. She thought he hadn't actually read the letters but of course he'd found them and read them when Emi was off washing her hair in a stream. He'd put them back carefully, so she wouldn't know. He was always prying into Emi's things, her thoughts and feelings too. It had started when they were little, and he'd riffle through her personal stuff, even her private treasure box full of pebbles and arrowheads. She'd bit him when she'd discovered that, sunk her strong teeth into his upper arm and refused to let go as he'd screamed. And left a mark that had taken days to fade. He'd been careful to wear sleeves over it. He didn't want Emi to get into trouble, and violence was strictly forbidden at Golden.

Maybe she'd bite him again, if she knew about the letters. He laughed to himself. At least he knew what that look was on her face and knew it wasn't his fault, not anything he had done. Why hadn't it cheered her up to know Tessa wanted her, loved her? Well, because it was sad, a missed opportunity. And it made Maira seem evil, truly the bad guy.

Well, he told himself, just more proof of lies, of the endless lies of Golden. And, he vowed, he was going to find Tessa for Emi. Albuquerque might be a huge and unfamiliar place, but he was good at figuring things out. Very good, in fact. He was going to do that for Emi.

Tessa, 2056

Tessa often thought about killing herself. Falling asleep, waking up in the middle of the night, sometimes even over breakfast. She thought about how she'd do it. She wasn't going to shoot herself. At Golden she'd been taught care and respect for guns. She'd been a soldier. She wasn't going to contaminate a tool she trusted.

Pills seemed the logical way. You could simply off yourself with enough over-the-counter acetaminophen. And she was a nurse practitioner... she could prescribe. Secanol washed down with tequila should do it—although she really didn't drink.

Sometimes she thought about starving herself. Not eating, withering away in plain sight. Every so often she'd try that, but would stall out at a few days' diet or cleanse. She couldn't go all the way down.

The thought of Paulus held her back. It would devastate him, and that wasn't fair or right. It would fuck Crystal up badly, too, even after all these years. And what about her staff? They'd blame themselves for not noticing or end up hating her.

If she killed herself, she'd be abandoning old Mrs. Gonzalez to her diabetes, sweet-faced Lydia to a difficult third trimester, lonely Fred to his hives. And so many others that she cared for with their cancer recurrences, their anxiety, their lack of medical services. Sure, there were other neighborhood health clinics, but this one was hers. Her little piece of the suffering world that she could try and help.

After all, she'd fought for a better world. She'd certainly tried, but sadly that had not really happened.

It was the same old world, minus a police state and a Tyrant: maybe a world with more hope and more freedom, and yet with the same problems.

And so Tessa's life went on. Tempted by death, but not completely.

Death with dignity was now legal in New Mexico. But Tessa couldn't exactly tell a doctor—I need a lethal dose because… I've fucked up really badly.

Where does it hurt?

That is what Tessa would have asked a patient.

It hurt everywhere, not just in her body but in the sky at sunset, the mountains turning red, mountains named for watermelons or blood.

This pain was from war. And leaving the Commune of the Golden Sun. And Emi, most of all Emi.

One other thing tied Tessa to life. That was her father, of course. Sometimes Paulus reminded Tessa of her dad, Jake. After all, they both limped. Jake always claimed he'd lost a wrestling match with an angel. When she was little, she'd almost believed it.

Now when she saw him she nagged about PT and meds for the arthritis. He'd just laugh and say, "Aspirin and the cane work for me. And you should have seen the other guy. His wings were shedding feathers by the time he took off."

Tessa saw her father regularly, if on the sly. All the pleas of her letters had fallen on Maira's deaf ears, but Jake had called her on a borrowed cell phone from town as soon as he had learned that Tessa was alive.

They'd see each other once a season. He'd walk out of Golden, she'd pick him up on the county road. She'd gotten him a cheap cell phone so he could call her. Golden felt remote, but nothing was remote anymore.

He'd stay with them in Albuquerque. He and Paulus got on easily. Tessa would treat him...movies, Thai food, Balloon Fiesta. He didn't watch television or news or inquire about new technology. He kept to the purity of Golden. Still, these visits with his daughter helped him keep going.

Jake would claim to Golden that he was out alone in the desert, doing sweats for his leg.

Of course he'd never take a gift back, but he kept some nice sweaters and shirts at Tessa's. And he brought her detailed news of Emi.

Jake was an old man now, his dark face wrinkled, his smile congenial. At heart he was still a math teacher, just hoping to make the world a better place through a little logical understanding.

He was another reason she wouldn't kill herself, a good reason.

Then, in the spring of 2056, something odd occurred. Tessa began to have a sensation—a forceful one—that something or someone was headed towards her. At first she assumed this was a premonition about a car wreck and was careful at intersections. Then she tried to ignore it, but the feeling grew more intense.

Every so often, Tessa would try and keep a diary. She'd get a pretty notebook and record weather (always too hot) and food and her mood. After a few days, she'd neglect to write—eventually just putting the journal in a drawer and forgetting all about it.

Now she went rummaging for a blank book and pulled out one with lined pages and a mottled purple design on the cover.

She wrote on the first page: Emi is headed for me.

Jake 2002-2026

Jake loved Golden; it was one of his few pure loves. Sometimes he felt he wasn't very good at love. Romance, long-term relationship, eluded him. And now that he was an old man, it was unlikely to show up.

He was, in his own way, a good father and grandfather. He'd loved Tessa when she was born, when she was little, lively and curious as a kitten. Then he'd almost lost her, when Maira had threatened him when he was leaving Vegas. And the truth was, he'd been willing to give Tessa up for Golden. Maira was such a... he didn't like the word bitch, but privately he had to admit—Maira could be a bitch.

Then he'd gotten lucky. Maira had changed her mind and brought Tessa to Golden. Jake had first seen Golden when he was eighteen. He was just an ordinary kid—good at math, wrestling team, Pittsburgh. It was the 1990s. His grandparents had cared passionately about civil rights and the fight for racial justice. His parents had cared too, of course, but were focused on their careers. He was raised with idealism and some pressure to be a professional. He didn't get into his first-choice college. Friends were driving to New Mexico. He went along, visited a commune out of curiosity. It sounded quaint, so old-fashioned. That was Golden.

He thought he'd stay forever.

He loved having his own little room, a tiny outbuilding. He really loved the food: fresh produce, real cream. He took to it all, learning to repair machinery and to bake.

Then the letters started. His folks were worried.

The pressure was on. They asked to meet him in Albuquerque at a nice hotel. Then, what they thought of as deprograming him began. What was he doing with his life? His grandparents hadn't fought so hard for him to be some kind of hippie, and a very out-of-date one at that.

And Jake had to admit it: after a few years at Golden, some disillusionment had set in. A failed love affair, then another. The lack of intellectual stimulation. Mostly everyone else was white. The endless, contentious meetings. Could Golden support another cat? This kind of question could tie things up for weeks.

And so he caved. Went back to what his parents considered to be the real world. Got a Master's Degree, dropped out of a Ph.D. program at the University of Nevada, and went to work teaching algebra at one of the Las Vegas community college campuses.

That's where he met Maira.

Jake still loved Golden, the memory of it, but now he loved teaching math. He couldn't really explain it. From the outside it looked like a grind, particularly the grading. But up close, it was dynamic. He'd look at their faces that first day of class. The students' expressions ranged from indifference to terror. No one was there by choice.

Algebra was simply a requirement for a nursing degree, micro-chip engineering, even culinary arts. But then he experienced the rush of seeing some people truly get it.

Almost everyone replaced their paralyzing fear with a bit of curiosity, a bit of desire to at least understand. And then the semester was over, and the cycle began again.

And there was Maira: a competent student, pretty, a bit mean. She was sarcastic, flirtatious, and absent-minded, as if she couldn't focus on another person for very long. Once class ended (she got an A-) they started dating, liking and hating each other from day to day. How they could have produced Tessa—so tough and lovely, so sincere and driven—was a mystery to both of them.

Then the world seemed to be ending. A failed election, with a Tyrant refusing to resign. Food shortages, armed gangs, no more workable cell towers. It became obvious to Jake that he needed to go back to Golden. His folks were dead. There was nothing to stop him. Except Maira waving a knife, so he wouldn't snatch Tessa, as if he was capable of something like that.

He'd fumed as he'd driven east. Did Maira really think so poorly of him? Then gotten distracted by how ominous the highway seemed. First he saw abandoned cars on the shoulder. They looked old and rusty. Had they always been there? Then, far ahead, he saw flares and flashing lights. It looked like a barricade. A line of traffic was forming. He veered off at the next exit, and went south. He'd shunpike after that.

He was set up for camping, and one night he pitched his tent near the pebbly wash on a fork of the Little Colorado. He lit a small fire, warmed up dinner, and sat content. Then he saw a man, a dark figure, walking towards him.

"Hey, good evening," Jake said. But the stranger did not respond, even when Jake offered him some toast and beans.

The stranger was naked to the waist. He grabbed Jake in an opening wrestler's hold.

The muscle memory came back to Jake, even though it was decades since he'd wrestled, and then he'd been young and skinny. The stranger was about Jake's height, and although he was a good wrestler, for some mysterious reason Jake could hold his own.

They wrestled all night, until the first light of dawn. "At least tell me your name," Jake said. It was like a one-night stand. It didn't seem right to share that kind of intimacy without knowing the other person's name.

"Your name is Jake," said the stranger, and he put a hand on Jake's femur and dislocated the left hip.

Then he turned and walked away.

Once the angel had left, Jake broke camp and limped to the car. The pain was close to unbearable. He took a dozen Advil and two edibles. He managed to drive. Thank God it wasn't a standard. He didn't have to use his injured left leg. He found the ER in the next small Arizona town. There was no wait that early in the morning. They popped the joint back in, gave him more serious painkillers, and said that he needed physical therapy, a lot of it. And if it didn't heal properly, maybe surgery.

He just kept driving until he reached Golden.

Of course the stranger was an angel. What else could he be? A hallucination didn't put out your hip. Jake's parents weren't very religious, but he'd been to church many times with his grandmother. He understood certain things, like calculus, and didn't understand others, like the appearance of an angel of God. However, he was far from arrogant and could accept what he could never explain.

When Jake got out of the car at Golden, the first person he saw ran towards him. It was an old buddy of his who'd been the kitchen manager and taught him to bake biscuits. Jake couldn't believe the guy was still there. They'd seen each other when Jake and Maira had visited that one time. It seemed so long ago. Now Jake was back for good, not just a visit.

They grabbed each other in a huge hug, and Jake leaned against the guy's neck, sobbing. He was home.

Emi, 2056

It took two nights out from the ruined city, but late in the afternoon of the third day, Matteo called a conference in the shade of a big globe willow, growing by a trickle of a stream. They'd been trekking over terrain that was still familiar: junipers and piñon trees, sagebrush, a few early spring flowers. They crossed some other trails, too. Deer had made some of these, but there were also some rutted muddy roads that held the tracks of tires. These roads didn't seem to lead anywhere in particular, but there were more of them.

"We're getting close," Matteo said. "And I think we better talk about how we're going to handle Blue Arrow before we get there."

"Why do we have to 'handle' it?" Madden asked.

"Well, it's an unknown, there are going to be a lot of people there…people we don't know…strangers. It's not like we have a lot of experience with this kind of thing." It wasn't like Matteo to sound so uncertain, and it made the rest of them nervous.

"We should stick together," Madden said. Emi nodded.

"No," said Co, "that doesn't work for me. This is supposed to be an adventure, a new experience. Not same old, same old. I think each person should be on their own, do whatever they want."

Emi shot a look at Matteo. She didn't want him off by himself, doing whatever he wanted with people—girls—who weren't her. "Hmm," she said, trying to not show her reaction.

The four of them looked at each other. It's starting, Matteo thought, we're going to split up once we reach this new world. At least I got us this far.

It's starting, Co thought, my life, my real life. What took so long? I can't wait!

It's ending, Madden thought, this comfy, cozy crew. I'll be back alone, heartbroken over Sarah...but she couldn't quite get the emotion of loss to rise.

I hate Matteo, Emi thought. He wants to fuck other people. I'll kill him, I'll fuck other people...more than he could imagine, I'll torture him with jealousy, I'll drive him insane.

"OK," Matteo said. "People have somewhat different needs. Co needs freedom to explore. Maddy needs security. And Emi and I will work out what we need together. We're a team."

Emi smiled at him and forgot all about torturing him.

Matteo continued, "So I have a proposal. We go in together. Then we set a time and meeting place. It could be hours, it could be days, we just have to agree. If it is weird and stupid, hours. If it is amazing, days. Then we meet up again and evaluate what we want to do. But take care of yourselves when you are on your own. Don't get in with drugs or sex you can't handle. Don't fight."

"Fight?" Madden was surprised.

"Yes, fight," Matteo said. "This isn't Golden. This is like the real world, or something. People fight. They hit each other, or shoot each other, or say horrible things."

"What should we do if that happens?" Madden sounded faint.

"Walk away," said Co, and Matteo nodded. "And we'll have our safe place. We'll set up a camp, the place to meet. And you can go there before, if there is any trouble."

"Good," said Emi. "This makes sense to me. I'm in."

They decided to sleep out one more night, and show up fresh at Blue Arrow in the morning, ready for the future.

Emi and Matteo sat up late, wrapped in a sleeping bag. "You were good," she said, "working things out for us. You understood each person."

"Thanks," he nodded. "But what do you want?"

"I want you to not fuck a lot of other people and drive me insane," she said.

Matteo started laughing. "That's what you're afraid of? Wow. Emi, I'm flattered. But really I'm a lot more worried that someone will get hurt, or there will be a big misunderstanding, and we won't know how to act, and we'll look like idiots, or worse, or...."

"I want you to not fuck a lot of other people and drive me insane," she said again.

"I promise. What about just a few people or make you just a little bit insane?" She hit his arm, almost hard enough to not be teasing.

"Ow," he said. "Emi, what are you so worried about?"

"I have this feeling," she said. "I have this feeling about this Blue Arrow place. That I have to go there before I look for my mother. At first it felt like a waste of time or something. I just wanted to go to Albuquerque. But now I think...I have to do this... something. And that I kind of have to do it by myself. And so I need to know you'll be there, later."

"Emi," he said, "I'll be there. Always. Remember when we were little?"

"Of course," she said and squeezed his hand.

"Did all of you get to say good-bye?" Madden suddenly blurted out the question loudly, interrupting Emi and Matteo's confab. They'd thought she was asleep, but apparently something on her mind was keeping her awake.

Emi didn't understand at first. "Good-bye to what?" she asked.

"To Golden. Of course. What else?"

The three of them looked at her, surprised.

"It honestly didn't occur to me," said Matteo. "I mean, my mom is my mom, still my mom, but for a long time...." He trailed off, but he didn't need to finish. They knew the story. A step-dad he didn't much like, the younger sibs who took all her time, her bad memories of Matteo's dad, who had left years ago and who had, she said, *been too smart for his own good.* Something that no doubt Matteo himself had inherited.

Generally he avoided them. Even at a small place like Golden that was possible, except on a big group day like Solstice. And then he barely would say hello.

"Of course I did," said Co. "I wrote my folks a letter explaining about the nest, how it split. And how I had to go. And that I love them, and I thanked them for raising me. And told them not to worry and that I'd be in touch when I could." Co left out feeling guilty about not saying good-bye in person and essentially just sneaking off.

"In touch?" Emi scoffed. "With Golden? They won't let you back in, or take a call, or a letter, and I know all about that!"

"Things change. My parents are good people," Co said serenely. Had Co always been this calm? Emi felt a rush of envy. If only she could be more like that.

"What about you, Emi?" Madden wanted to know. "Did you say good-bye? To Maira?"

"Yes," said Emi. "Kind of. I sort of left her a message." Like stealing all her money and fancy earrings and letters. My letters, she corrected herself silently.

"What about your grandpa?"

"Jake? Well, I thought about it, but it seemed safer not to. And I have the weirdest feeling I'm going to get to see him, sometime soon, anyway."

"That's weird," Madden echoed.

"Life is generally weird," said Co. "Let's get organized."

No one had asked Madden if she had said good-bye. There was no one for her to say good-bye to. Her mom was dead. Madden had never known her father. Her mom had "left" Madden to Golden. They were her guardians. And then she'd loved Sarah.

But Golden had guarded her too well. And she'd had to go.

Matteo directed them, and the next day they arrived at what was obviously the right place. A huge blue arrow—point down—looked as if it had been shot into the earth. It was metal, and the paint was peeling. Despite its decay, it still had an impressive presence. Behind it was a U-shaped row of doors, each appearing to lead into a separate room. A big sign, corroded and cracked, read THE BLUE ARROW MOTEL. VACANCY. Matteo could see that at one time the sign had had neon tubes that lit up. No more.

The pavement was buckling. Tumbleweed filled a corner. Still, Co couldn't help feeling a kind of charm —all those doors, all those windows, right next to each other. Golden would have enjoyed a set-up like that.

"Stop," Co's internal voice instructed. Not everything was now compared to Golden.

See this now. Golden is gone. Left behind.

Madden didn't like the arrow. Obviously it was fake, but even so, it looked like the building had almost been hit, been destroyed, as if by a meteor from space.

Emi felt distracted, hot and itchy. She worried she was getting a yeast infection. She worried…was Matteo happy to be here? What about Co? Had Madden really gotten over her heartbreak? Was that an early mosquito bite on her arm, was anything else worth worrying about?

Then something happened, and all of them froze where they were.

Music. Loud. Rhythmic. Almost shaking the earth. Seeming to shake the air. Melody, floated on top, urgent, metallic. A voice singing louder than any voice they had ever heard. Encouraging them to come closer to its source.

"Hang on a sec," Matteo said. "Things are starting to happen. Better pick a place to meet up again." He pointed to a bunch of dead trees clustered around an empty stock tank just to the left of the motel. "Meet here again in—how long?"

"Tonight?" Madden tried.

"Two days from now," said Co.

"Let's say, not tonight, but tomorrow night. At moonrise. I'm going to mark the spot with my sleeping bag." Matteo tossed it.

"Won't someone steal it?" Madden worried.

"Naw, I don't think so. Plus it's pretty ratty."

They all noted the exact location of where they'd meet again. And between now and then, anything could happen.

Then they moved forward. Stopped. Then at last ran. There was a huge rectangular hole cut in the ground, made of cement, empty and sunburnt, painted a peeling blue.

For skateboards? The kids had built structures like that at Golden once. Was it a pond that had been drained? Matteo pulled something out from a long-ago picture book. A swimming pool. Once filled with water. Empty now. No, not empty. A half dozen people with instruments were playing, reverb echoing off the walls. Somehow it was electronic, the sound amplified. Two guitars, a bigger stringed instrument, drums: very loud drums. And a singer: a short, skinny girl in a purple tank top, bangs in her eyes. Singing, no, wailing, like the wind, like…. Matteo's ability to process wobbled, then came to a complete stop. He was just whisked away, on gigantic wings of sound.

Madden started tearing up. She'd never heard anything like this before. The music was telling her a story, about how her mother had loved her when she was a baby.

About how Sarah had also really loved her, until she'd stopped. How Golden was shining, but receding behind her into the distance. How a woman was waiting for her, and a new place. She started sobbing hysterically.

Emi threw her arms around Madden. She was hearing things in the music too.

Only Co was not stunned by the sound. Co walked forward. There was a flight of metal steps leading down into the pool. Co easily took the little jump at the end. Emi suddenly saw Co as others might—tall, lanky, tousle-haired. Co was a boy, then a girl, then both, then neither. But not really fixed, all of that could change. Maybe just a tall, lanky, tousle-haired ...person. A person who, walking with a purposeful stride, headed towards the musicians. Picked up a tambourine, and started shaking it.

That's it, Emi thought. Co was gone. Into a new world. And what about her, Emi, and Matteo, and Madden?

"Hey, welcome," a voice said. They looked up. A woman of about twenty, wearing a brightly tie-dyed T-shirt, held out her hand to shake. Matteo took it and shook it rather heartily. He'd read about this. It was a friendly custom. Emi was impressed. She and Madden were just staring.

"OK. Welcome," the woman said again. "I'm a marshal. There are a bunch of us around, same T-shirt." She gestured. "If you have questions or problems, just ask." They stared. They had questions, but no one could ask. She smiled. "You all from around here?"

They kept staring; finally Madden managed to whisper. "We're from Golden, the Commune of the Golden Sun."

"Sure. Good."

"You've heard of it?"

"Sure. It isn't far from here," she gestured vaguely west. "Everyone knows about it around here. The commune that shut its doors."

"Well, yes," said Matteo. "Can you explain a little

bit about Blue Arrow? This place?"

"Sure thing. That's what I'm here for. Obviously Blue Arrow was once a motel. The rooms are kind of decrepit, but you are welcome to crash if one is empty. The band is out there." She gestured, self-evidently, to the pool. "There will be music all the time, a long lineup, probably a few days of music, back to back. It can be hard to sleep. You've got earplugs?"

They shook their heads. "Music is good," Emi said, sounding embarrassingly moronic to herself. It wasn't easy to talk to someone she hadn't known her whole life.

"And then," the marshal said, "there's the Ziggurat. It's, well, it's a lot of things." She pointed to some tumbledown buildings about a five-minute walk from the pool. "It's got hot springs and, well, a bunch of other stuff too. Most of it is underground. It doesn't look like anything from here. But it is pretty, well, amazing. You may have to split up though, to get inside, they don't usually.... You'll just have to see when you get there."

"What is a ziggurat thing?" Madden asked.

"It's a pyramid with steps," said Matteo, that pleased-with-himself look on his face.

"In Egypt?"

"No, more like Mesopotamia."

"This place is right here. It's just a name," said Emi. She didn't like the sound of any of it. "Let's go." And get it over with, she added silently.

"Well, good luck," said the marshal. She was helpful, Emi thought, but she sounded so vague, just saying well and OK all the time.

"Bye. Thanks so much."

"You're welcome. Bye."

The three of them headed towards the Ziggurat, whatever that was. There was a red neon sign, OFFICE. They went down a little flight of steps into a small, bland space that looked like a waiting room. A tall black woman sat behind a desk. She had golden fingernails and glittery eye shadow. She was wearing a short, black, silk dress. She looked majestic, and not like she was at a hippie party in the desert.

"Yes?" she said, showing little interest.

"We want to come in," Emi said. Matteo and Madden nodded.

"You have the fee?"

They looked blank.

"A dollar in change each. That is kind of antique in today's world, but that is the fee." Emi's heart sank. That was impossible. She was afraid to go in, but now that she couldn't, she wanted to.

"Hang on," Madden said. She started rummaging through her backpack, producing a ball of twine, a box of crackers, antibiotic ointment, a pack of cards, and a little velvet bag. It contained all kinds of dirty silver-colored coins.

"My God," said Matteo, stunned. Madden just smiled and paid the woman.

"OK," the woman put the money in the box. "Here are the rules. No pets. No children. And don't act like either."

"Anything we should expect?" Emi asked.

"It is against the rules for me to tell you," the woman said, and waved her hand dismissively.

They exited through a small metal door. There was another flight of steps, this one much longer, leading straight down. The steps looked like wood at first, then widened and seemed to be stone.

The space opened into a vast cavern. They saw before them a gigantic party in a gigantic pool of steaming water. A series of pools, actually, large and small, with sulfuric-smelling clouds rising from the contained clear blue water.

People were naked: dozens, maybe hundreds of people, soaking with their eyes closed or lounging, chatting quietly. There were alcoves for some privacy, and Emi averted her eyes. She'd seen people make love her whole life, but that didn't mean it didn't embarrass her.

Madden, not known for her modesty, stripped and stuffed her clothes into her pack. It was hot and humid, and of course the water looked inviting. Matteo took off his shirt.

His eye was caught by a particular pool, off to one side, with a cool-looking mosaic on the bottom, a woman whose hair was turning into snakes. The people in the pool were obviously very high on something: tripping, staring at things no one else could see or engrossed, looking at their own hands.

He nudged Emi, "I want what they're doing."

"I thought you said we were a team."

"Always, Emi, always." But his attention was off her. "Come with me," he offered.

"Absolutely not. I'm not about to drop some hallucinogen with weird strangers in a super-weird place."

"OK," he said. "You know where we are supposed to meet. Bye. I love you."

The mosaic pool pulled him. A friendly-looking guy gave him a small wave, uncurling his hand to reveal a stash of pills and mushrooms.

"Is there any LSD?" Matteo asked.

The guy smiled and pointed. Matteo went for it. Mushrooms were commonplace at Golden, but acid was not. He'd only had it once and was ready for more. Matteo loved drugs. He wasn't in charge for the moment, and this was his adventure.

He swallowed, following bits of advice... don't mix this with anything, give it a half hour at least, don't take any more, and *stay hydrated.* There was a fountain of cool, fresh water right nearby. Matteo filled his bottle, put his pack where he could see it, and settled in.

"I really do love you, Emi," he said, as if she was right next to him. But she wasn't.

"It's just us," Madden said, and she and Emi started sobbing and hugging each other.

Both of them knew they couldn't stay together for long, but they clung to the moment.

A large door, painted hot pink with black ravens, seemed to lead from the main area to somewhere quieter. Madden went first, then Emi followed.

It was a long, winding corridor with lots of little rooms off of it. Everything was brightly painted— green zebra stripes, huge flowers and tiny people, trees with faces, rainbows in sparkly colors. It was lit from above, maybe through high windows, but the effect was dim. Curtains hung on the doorways of numerous small rooms, and the sound of water dripping was everywhere.

An old woman was sitting on a metal folding chair outside one of the curtained rooms in a faded housedress and hairnet. She caught Madden's wrist.

"I've drawn a bath for you," she said.

"Sure. We'd love a bath," Madden said.

"Just for one. You," said the old woman.

Emi and Madden looked each other. The look said—well, this is it.

"You know where to meet," Emi said.

"Yeah, I do."

"Yeah, OK," Emi said.

"See you there," Madden mouthed.

The old woman pulled her in, and she disappeared from Emi's sight.

Emi had never felt so alone—alone alone—in her entire life. And she was disappointed, as she wanted to soak too. I'll take my own bath, she told herself, and kept walking. Fuck everyone. They were all off on their own adventures. Well, she could have one too.

Madden saw an enormous old-fashioned bathtub, with a continuous stream running into it from an open faucet. It must have been draining somehow, because it didn't overflow. There was a chair, and she put her pack on it to keep it dry.

The water was the perfect temperature. Hot, but not too hot. Silky to the touch. A faint smell of minerals, but that was to be expected. A gentle steam rose, filling the air with moisture that then condensed and trickled down the walls.

She slipped in, relaxed. The muscles in her legs let go, and her calves softened. Her neck stopped feeling like a rock from the pressure of the pack. She could sense the old woman sitting outside, protecting her. She hadn't felt that safe, watched over, in a long time. Madden sank into the water up to her neck. She saw her feet wiggling, seemingly very far away.

Shapes began to emerge in the water. She saw herself as a baby, passed from arm to arm, lap to lap. Toddling forward and meeting… Emi, of course, who, the story went, took a piece of chewed gooey something out of her own mouth and stuck it in Madden's.

When she was little, even if people called her Maddy she knew Madden was her full name. She had no last name, and she wondered if that was going to be a problem out in the world. The big world? Was it the so-called real world?

It certainly didn't feel real yet.

She saw herself growing up in the nest. Emi and Matteo. Matteo and Emi, like one person. She remembered how Matteo got scratched by barbed wire when Emi was chasing him. How scared they'd been by the blood. Emi wanted to get Maira, but Matteo didn't want that. It was Madden who'd patched him up. It had healed well. Years later Emi told her it was a scar only the size of a pinkie fingernail.

And then she, Madden, had grown up in a way that was her own, on her forays camping out of Golden. Limiting herself to water and string, going one day, two days, on forage. Trying to manage without a hat *(terrible sunburn and migraine)*. Catching snakes and smuggling them home *(about fifty percent successful)*. Staying up all night, talking to the moon...all her private experiences.

And then Sarah, who had wiped Madden's mind of everything else. And how that wasn't good. She could see that now. And more than that, when she probed the ache in her heart left by Sarah, she couldn't quite find it. She remembered kissing Sarah, those long, slow, endless kisses, just to see if she could evoke the pain of loss. But it was gone. Could the heart finally heal, like a skinned knee? And like the knee, still look a little tender but actually feel fine?

Emi used to say: "Maddy, you are the weirdest mix—brave and scaredy cat, needy and strong. You confuse me."

But, Madden reassured herself. Only yesterday Emi had said: "Madden, you are the greatest packer on earth! You have everything. You are so prepared." And that was even before the pile of change.

Madden sighed. That reminded her that she had lavender shampoo. She got out of the tub, retrieved it, and lathered her hair in lovely scented bubbles.

What else? She could bake, garden, weld, cook, take care of kids, sew, knit, mend, weave, butcher, roof, do first aid, drive a tractor, plaster, and keep chickens and goats. She could do math—Emi's grandpa had seen to that. She could make love unselfishly, be a friend, and catch any wild creature. Surely there was a place for her, wherever she was going.

She heard a tap on the wall—the old woman asking for entry. "Sure, come on in," Madden called.

"I can give you a wrap," the woman said. Madden wasn't sure exactly what that meant but got out of the tub and followed to another small room. There was a narrow table, and when Madden climbed onto it, the old woman told her to lie down on a sheet and then wrapped her tightly in it. She then covered Madden with a scratchy blanket and wrapped her head in a towel, partially covering her face. Madden had barely murmured a thank you when she felt herself drifting off into deep sleep.

When she awakened, she had to pee violently and had a raging thirst. Her eyeballs were gritty. Luckily there was a toilet in the next cubicle. How long had she slept? Might it be longer than one night, more like two? Was that possible? She couldn't tell anything by the dim light. She sucked on her water bottle and put her clothes on. Her stomach cramped with hunger, and she allowed herself a little snack. She'd eat more once she got out of here.

Retracing her steps, Madden soon found the pink door and was back in the cavernous room of pools. There was almost no one there and no sign of Matteo, tripping or otherwise. Outside, the dim light might have been dusk or dawn, but the stars were slowly vanishing—dawn. But which dawn? What day was it? Not that Madden had kept track of the days of the week on their journey.

The air was moist, and birds were starting to sing. Back beneath the dead tree by the empty tank she saw two lumps, which proved to be Matteo and his gear. He was dead asleep, not even in his sleeping bag but with his head propped on it like a pillow. So they were early, and the others would be back by moonrise that night?

Despite everything, Madden was exhausted, and she had to pee again, which she took care of behind a bush. She had breakfast—supper?—from her stores of dried meat and fruit and nuts. She drank more water. She made camp and got into her sleeping bag.

When she woke again, whatever night it was, the moon was rising, and Matteo, Emi, and Co were sitting around a small fire, talking softly. Their familiar shapes and voices flooded her with a sense of security, even if she suspected it wasn't going to last.

After Madden had been pulled out of the corridor by the old lady, Emi had kept going. She had understood what Matteo had said about a ziggurat, although all of this just looked like hot springs. She walked—it must have been a half a mile or more—in the twisty, dimly lit corridor. It narrowed for a bit and then opened up again, and eventually it ended at one side of a vast space.

Emi stopped and looked around cautiously. She appeared to be inside some kind of stepped pyramid that was partially sunken into the earth on its lower levels. It had an enormous square base that translated into an echoing empty space as Emi crossed it. There were hanging globe lights that cast too many shadows for her comfort. It was like crossing a city plaza late at night, empty except for a stray cat or two. Of course Emi had never actually seen such a place. Maybe in a dream or in a book?

At what she thought was the west end of the square was the beginning of a huge ramp, inclining upwards at a gentle slant. It was built of bricks of a porous stone and some kind of dark wood.

Emi did not like being alone in this space. It reminded her of... but what could it possibly remind her of?

Then she realized it reminded her of the stories of the destruction of the world, the stories told to children at Golden, and the images she had seen in her mind's eye of those stories.

Maira had considered these apocalyptic tales to be perfectly acceptable bedtime stories. She'd tuck Emi in and tell her how the world outside of Golden was a desolate, burning desert, where rivers flamed, and poison fell from the sky. One night Jake and Maira were tucking her in together. Her grandparents must have been getting along better than usual. But then Maira had started in, and Jake had turned on his good heel and walked out with a disgusted expression. Emi hadn't realized it then, but he must not have approved of all the lying.

Maira had other stories, too, better ones. She, as well as Jake, had come from a place called Las Vegas, far to the west of Golden, but still a desert place, a hot place getting hotter. Maira had once told Emi about some kind of palace that was a pyramid of black glass, with a beacon of light shining from the top into the night sky and piercing the cosmos beyond. It was called the Luxor, which Emi assumed meant rich or luxurious. When you entered, you were greeted by huge golden statues of an ancient king. Emi was pretty vague on geography. She had no idea where this kingdom was.

Maira said it was ruled by Pharaoh. Probably it was farther out in the desert and maybe a long time ago.

"My mom worked there for a while," Maira had said.

"What did she do?"

"She helped people gamble."

"What is that?"

"Throwing away their money," Maira's expression hardened.

"Why?" It didn't make sense. But Maira had stiffened and wouldn't say any more. Then, as if responding to a question, Maira had said, "She died, and it fell to ruins." Emi had stayed still and quiet until Maira had walked away.

There were no statues of Pharaoh here, although presumably a ziggurat was the kind of place that Pharaohs might like.

After waiting a long moment, Emi began to make her way up the ramp. The incline wasn't bad, and her legs were tough after days of walking, but she did not go quickly. She was afraid, and with no one else to observe her, she could admit it freely.

What could she expect? She hoped it wasn't going to be a riddle or a test. Her grandfather had taught her the riddle of the sphinx. He liked it because he walked with a cane.

What exactly was a sphinx? Hadn't Maira mentioned that there was a golden statue of one in the Luxor? It had the body of a lion, the head of a man, and the wings of a falcon. Emi had never seen a lion, of course, but she'd seen plenty of falcons, mostly peregrines.

And what was the riddle?

What goes on four legs in the morning, two legs at noon, three legs at night? She knew the answer. A person.

That is, a baby crawled on four legs. A grown-up walked on two. And an old person, who needed a cane, walked on three.

She hoped she wouldn't meet a terrible beast who would quiz her on algebra, or ask her a knock-knock joke.

Knock-knock. Who's there? No one.

The ramp led higher and higher. She began to see what looked like clouds brushing against the ceiling. But that wasn't possible. Nor were the crows who seemed to be flying about. The top of the dome, for that is what appeared to cap the huge building she was climbing inside of, might just be painted like the sky. Or maybe there was a hole in it, through to the real sky.

At this distance, she couldn't tell. And kept walking.

Emi started to feel dizzy and a little sick. She came to a small door on the left-hand side of the ramp.

The doorknob was painted red. Emi opened it. Inside a room, it was snowing, and a large raven sat on a silver tree, cocked an eye at her, and cawed "Emi."

"That's me," she said.

"Good," said the raven. And then, "Go find your mother."

"But where is she?" Emi asked.

And the raven was gone.

After that, things began to happen fast. There were dozens of doors, and Emi started opening them but not entering the rooms. One was full of blown up balloons—there'd been a few at Golden—all white, all floating upwards. The next room opened to a space that was cold and pitch black. Emi shut that door fast.

But the next few rooms seemed meant for her, personally, even if she couldn't quite read the message. Behind a door painted with a pleasant scene of a farm, Emi saw a woman washing dishes at an old sink. The woman looked faded, if still young. She'd once been fair-haired, but now all the color was washed out of her. She wore a dress with front snaps. She was looking out the open window. Some very pretty red roses were in full bloom. Emi could smell their sweetness, but the woman did not smile.

"Hi," Emi said.

"Emi, come to me. I'm your mother," the woman said.

"No you're not," Emi said. She shut the door, but somehow felt wistful.

Then, behind a door painted shiny black, Emi saw another woman sitting at a kitchen table, playing solitaire. The woman looked tired and rubbed her back a few times as if it ached. She was wearing jeans that were too tight for her plump figure and a silky purple shirt with a gaudy design. She placed the Queen of Spades on the King of Hearts. She looked up, right at Emi, and gave her a wink.

"Are you my grandmother?" Emi asked.

"Maybe yes. Maybe no. How is Maira?" the woman asked.

"Maira is a bitch," Emi answered.

The woman laughed, low in her throat. "That is true. And you must be Emi."

"Maybe yes and maybe no." Emi turned and shut the door as she walked on.

Emi opened the neighboring door. A tall Black woman had her back to the door. She was painting on an easel. The picture showed a woman in an African-looking caftan of bright colors. Her head was elegantly wrapped in a scarf with the same pattern. Emi wanted to say hello, but she didn't want to interrupt the painter. She stood watching, and then the woman turned to her and smiled. "Travel safely," the woman said, so Emi waved and moved on.

At the next door, Emi hesitated, then turned the knob of turquoise stone. There, a woman was bending over a bed in a dimly lit room. There was a figure beneath the covers, slight and thin. The woman straightened up and turned to look at Emi. It was Maira. Emi slammed the door shut, heart pounding. She stood outside the door, stricken. Was that really Maira? Of course it couldn't be. Maira was still at Golden. And who was the person so still beneath the blankets? It had looked to be a girl.

If Emi was honest, it had looked to be Emi herself lying in the bed.

"Enough of this fucking shit," Emi said out loud. Behind each door there was yet another mother. But none of them was Tessa, the only one that Emi wanted. Above her, clouds and crows swirled, although she seemed no closer to the ceiling.

There was one more door. It had a good feeling... pale green with big pink flowers.

She opened it, tumbled forward, fell through empty space, and landed gently on a sleeping bag at the meeting place by Blue Arrow.

Emi was dazed. For a long moment, it was as if she was deaf. She couldn't hear anything at all—not the wind, or far-off music, or the beating of her own heart. The world was profoundly silent.

Everyone else was already there, and the moon was rising. "You snuck up on us!" Matteo said. "Did you have a good time?"

"What?" she asked. She could now hear his words, but she couldn't understand.

Was he speaking English? She couldn't tell. "Did you have fun?" Matteo asked again.

Fun? Emi looked at him incredulously. Had fun been the point? "It was like...more heavy than just ...fun," Emi said.

"Yeah," said Madden. "It was cool, and weird, and I met this old lady. And I think I'm over Sarah! But what happened, I can't really, like, explain it. Or talk about it."

"Me too," said Emi. "Matteo, you had fun?"

"Yup," he said. "Great drugs, nice people. Fun trip. Fun."

The conversation was going awkwardly, as if they didn't really know each other.

Maybe something had happened to drive them apart.

Then Co started talking: softly at first, then increasingly animatedly. "You know, I went into the pit and picked up a tambourine. Everyone was singing. I didn't know the song, but I started to learn it. After a couple of hours, I was pretty exhausted, but then this guy noticed I needed a change of pace." Co paused.

A guy? The thought startled Emi. Co had just said it in that overly casual way that meant something. Did Co look different? No, Co just looked like Co, still pushing brown curls off their face.

"So this guy," Co continued, "he just asked me, well, he offered a drum. Not a hand drum. A drum with sticks. Pedals. Kind of complicated. Kind of amazing. I can't even explain."

Out of the evening air, a figure appeared and sat down on the ground next to Co. "David, hi," Co said.

A shock wave ran through the group. This was real, different. It was the future.

Maira, 2056

At first, Golden was in shock at the departure of yet another four of its children. Matteo's mother alternated between sobbing and cursing him. Co's parents soon retreated from the emotional chaos and turned to each other for support. Only Maira seemed oddly calm.

Jake appeared worried. Yet he guessed that Emi was headed towards Tessa. He figured he'd hear about it soon. He was just wishing her and the other three well on their perilous journey. And maybe it wasn't so perilous. Maybe it would be for the best.

He watched Maira with concern. Why wasn't she yelling and threatening? "Maira, are you all right?" he asked tentatively.

She nodded. "It's fine. Emi is still here. She's just sick in bed in her room."

"Can I see her?" he asked gently.

Maira led him to the room, but the bed was empty.

"I'm taking care of her now," she told Jake in a soft voice.

When he reported on this to Golden, people were divided. Some felt it was a transitional thing and that Maira needed time to adjust. Some felt that Maira was having a break from reality and needed intervention. But as they couldn't come to a conclusion, they agreed to let some time pass.

Maira tended the sick girl, the pale thin girl, every day. The girl lay inert in Emi's bed. She was sick but she didn't die. And she did not get well. Maira changed her nightgown every day. When it was warm, she dressed her in a soft T-shirt and panties. She changed the sheets every week.

The girl could sit up if helped and sip water or weak tea. She could swallow applesauce and other soft foods. She could use a bedpan if aided. She grew very thin, and her hands were transparent. But she did not die.

"How is Emi?" people asked for the first weeks and months. If she was real, the medical team wanted to break protocol and smuggle her out. Take her to town... to a real doctor, to an expert, to a hospital in Albuquerque even. Or maybe, if Emi was a delusion, to take Maira to a psychiatric ward. But here they were stymied. Maira had moved Emi—real or imaginary—to a remote outbuilding and would let no one in.

Every time Maira asked the girl if she wanted to go, the girl shook her head.

She squeezed Maira's hand and implored her with huge eyes—eyes that had once been Emi's.

"You want to stay here?" Maira asked.

The girl nodded. She couldn't speak, but she could communicate with small gestures. She seemed to understand everything Maira told her. Soon, Maira felt she could read her mind. She'd turn the girl over, adjust the window shade.

People gossiped about Maira behind her back. They argued about what to do. But as days passed and became months, she stopped eating in the dining hall and took her meals on a tray in the girl's room. People began to forget about Maira, a bent, old-looking woman with a sick child. Or a dead child she was grieving? No one had seen Emi in a long time. Matteo and his crew were long gone. Golden had new leaders, new fights, new issues, new children. Were they too reliant on ethanol? Was there enough labor budget to replace all the roofs at the same time? Were there enough choices for the vegans at dinner? Could they keep another cat?

It wouldn't seem easy for Golden to forget Maira. But it was easier than fighting her.

Emi, 2056

Things change, then they don't, then they change back. However he looked at it, Matteo had to admit he wasn't really in charge. Yes, he'd gotten them out of Golden; he'd gotten them here, and safely. No one had as much as a scratch. But Matteo had seen things when he was tripping in the pool. Yes, they were the kind of things everyone saw tripping, but it was worth being reminded. He was a tiny speck. Shining like a star, but tiny. Everyone else was on their own path: everything else, from electron to supernova. He shook himself. This wasn't the time for a flashback, fun as that was.

He had to focus on being introduced to David, who in the past few hours had suddenly become the most important person in Co's universe. David was a tall, skinny gay guy, taller than Co, but somehow also looking like Co. And he and Co were talking, rapid-fire, about Albuquerque and music and something called the University of New Mexico, where David was something called a TA, and about scholarship money for people who hadn't gone to high school, and more.

Emi got it first. "Co, you are going to live with David?"

"Yes," Co said.

Emi opened her mouth, but no words came out. She closed it, and a small sound escaped, a sound almost of pain.

Madden looked at David and said brusquely: "Don't forget that Co has friends. If you fuck up or hurt Co, we will kill you."

Somehow that was the right thing to say, and everyone laughed. Madden looked surprised at her own success, then laughed too.

"It's just the three of us," Emi said the next morning. Madden and Matteo nodded. "One down, three to go," Matteo muttered.

"Please stop it," Emi said. She didn't want to think of the end of the journey but just keep walking. They crossed a flat plain, basin land really, with the sky above it a brilliant, cloudless blue arching over the grassland. Then, towards evening, they went up in altitude again; bigger trees, pines, the soft rustling of wind picking up. There was no obvious place to camp, which made Matteo nervous. He liked something—a feature—to mark the spot. He gave up, though, found a pleasant enough area, and built a fire. They ate early, and Matteo went off a bit from the others, unrolled his sleeping bag, and quickly fell asleep. Emi knew to leave him alone. Matteo was tired and in a way lonely without Co. With Co they could still pretend they were part of Golden, moving together. Now that was fading.

Emi and Madden sat looking into the fire, sharing a blanket. It was peaceful, if a bit melancholy.

"Feels kind of…wolf-y," Madden said.

"I doubt there are any lobos around here," Emi said.

"Weren't they reintroduced?" Madden asked.

Emi shrugged. That was the problem with education at Golden. It was so spotty you could never be sure if you'd actually learned something or if that thing was true. Grown-ups would get all excited about a subject and try to teach it until bored kids wandered off and even the would-be teacher just gave up.

"I can't believe Co left," said Madden.

"Found love," Emi said.

"Yes."

"Do you think that was what Co wanted all along?"

"I feel like Co started off just wanting to get out of Golden. But then found love."

"Isn't that good?" Emi asked.

"Not when it takes you away from your friends," Madden protested.

"Maybe your turn is coming," Emi said.

Madden brightened. "When? How?"

"Who can tell? But I still bet it is."

"I believe that, too," said Madden. She was pleasantly surprised to hear herself say that. She must really be over Sarah. And why not? A lot had happened.

"But what about me?" Emi wanted to know.

"You already have love!" Madden exclaimed.

"But what about, what am I going to find?"

"You know, I'm not a fortune teller," Madden said. "But I hope you find your mom."

The next day they continued to climb and then hit a dirt track, quite obviously a trail.

Matteo calculated that it was indeed leading them into town. Town. His normal enthusiasm quailed. People. Machines. Systems. Unfamiliar things. Who knew if they might be in some kind of trouble. He was a little sharp with Emi. Preoccupied with Madden.

"Chill," Madden whispered to Emi. "You know how he gets tense."

They crossed railroad tracks. Matteo noted that they were in use, not just abandoned. They came out of scrub and up a little rise and found themselves at a crossing of a two-lane highway. Matteo sat down suddenly, his knees giving way under his heavy pack. It was hot out, too hot for this time of year, with the sun climbing up in the sky.

"Matteo! Matteo!" Emi was shocked.

"I feel like I... I can't go first anymore. I think I was depending on Co. And then, those drugs were fabulous, but ever since I've felt a little woozy... I'm sorry."

Everyone knew he was lying. "He's afraid," Emi hissed into Madden's ear.

Unfazed, Madden stepped forward. "Follow me," she said.

Madden crossed the highway, and they followed. A few seconds later a truck whizzed by, going faster than anything they had ever seen. Emi felt wind against her cheeks.

A metal sign loomed up: WELCOME TO MOUNTAINVIEW. Population 820. Altitude 6,495.

"Is that high up?" Madden wanted to know.

"About five hundred feet higher than Golden," said Matteo, and the others felt relieved... he hadn't lost it entirely.

And then they were in the town. Later on it would be a private joke... how awed they'd been, overwhelmed by a little country town. But they were. There was a feed store, a small cafe, two churches, an old hotel that looked closed, and a large general store. A few big trees shaded some of the street, but mostly it was dry and dusty and overly warm.

"We should go in," Madden pointed her chin towards the general store. That's what it said, Cuzart's General Store, in peeling red letters on a sun-blasted sign.

The three of them stood stock-still. Emi could feel the earth turning, even if her feet were planted on it. The earth was a cold blue pebble in empty space.

It was not a good feeling.

When Emi came to, she was inside the store, lying on a blanket on the floor, with four worried faces hovering above her.

Later, everyone would remember it differently. Matteo had been worried, but not as worried as he should have been. He didn't realize that this was the start of something, the start of... well, how could he have? Even years later he wouldn't understand it completely. His understanding too was marred by guilt. After all, he was the one who took Emi away from Golden Sun. His mind would run on and on with this. No, he did not understand it.

For Madden, her startled fear for Emi turned swiftly into one of the great moments of her life. Probably *the* great moment, the most important one. For two figures ran out of the store to help them with Emi in the street. And one of those people was the most beautiful woman Madden had ever seen. She was Madden's age, but taller. She had long, curly black hair, a creamy brown complexion, and huge, caring eyes. Matteo saw a pretty but ordinary girl in jeans with a red shirt. Madden saw a goddess come to earth and her own future.

Madden smiled widely, probably inappropriately, over Emi's prone body.

"I'm Liz," the girl smiled back: a full, open, expectant smile. The two of them stood grinning foolishly at each other as if suddenly transported, oblivious to the reality before them.

The taller figure who had run to their aid introduced herself quite formally as Mrs. Sanchez, and told them to carry Emi in. She had not suddenly been struck by Cupid's arrow and was concerned and helpful.

"We should get her into bed," she told her daughter, Liz. "You have the key to the hotel?" Liz nodded, and a few minutes later they walked a shaky Emi, who had mostly come to, across the street and up the steps of the old hotel.

"The sheets are fresh in room 3," Mrs. Sanchez said.

Although the hotel was unused and locked, it was clean and dusted. In a parlor, light fell on old velvet and gilt chairs. The corridor was a little creepy, with blind turns and creaking floorboards. Room 3 seemed fine, with a nice rag rug and heavy curtains that Mrs. Sanchez tied back.

Emi lay under the covers, still feeling disoriented. Matteo sat holding her hand, offering her sips from his water bottle.

"Let's get something to eat," Mrs. Sanchez said. "Liz, Madden, I'll treat at the cafe. And bring Emi and Matteo back some takeout."

Emi said she wasn't hungry; Matteo said he could certainly eat pie... any kind was fine.

Madden found herself alone with Mrs. Sanchez and Liz, who seemed to sparkle with an inner radiance.

The cafe was just an ordinary place, although it took Madden a long time to realize that. You were given some folded sheets of paper that listed things to eat. There was a whole section for dessert. A few extra items were written on a blackboard. Then you picked what you wanted. A waitress came by and took your order. Then the food arrived, piping hot. Then you ate and paid but not in paper money. You used a plastic card. It was a system, and it fascinated Madden.

Then the dreaded questions began. "So, where are you kids from?"

"Well, it is a little hard to explain. Golden Sun. It's an umm... commune... west of here."

"Golden! Sure I know it. You were good customers for a lot of years. Then, was it the pandemic? The civil war? Things kind of shut down. I still do some big orders, but the same guy just comes a few times a year. And he doesn't talk to me. Not like the old days. They used to bring me beautiful fresh produce, particularly tomatoes. And sometimes preserves—delicious preserves, just to be neighborly." But Mrs. Sanchez trailed off, stopped by the look of sheer panic on Madden's face.

"Madden?" she asked. "You left? Why?"

But Madden couldn't really speak, because Liz had grabbed her hand under the table and was gently squeezing it with her own long warm fingers.

"Uh," Madden blushed from the pressure.

Mrs. Sanchez, not knowing the cause, tried to rescue her. "I'm sorry, hon. I didn't mean to pry. I'm sure you and your friends had your reasons. Places like Golden can be kind of claustrophobic. Sealed off from the rest of the world."

Madden nodded.

"Not like Mountainview is so cosmopolitan," Liz piped up.

"No. But we like it here." Mother and daughter smiled at each other. "Of course we need more help with the store. I'm just kind of overwhelmed with the ordering and accounts. Liz, you're good with customers but not great when it comes to the bank."

"Mom, stop it. We don't even know Madden, and already you are complaining and going down your worry list, just like you do."

Mrs. Sanchez looked squarely at Madden. "I'm looking to hire. What can you do?"

"Do?"

"What are your skills?"

"Well, I can raise chickens, herd, drive a tractor, weld, bake, brew, take care of babies, use first aid. I can identify plants, hunt, fish, do basic farm machinery repairs, drive, sew, and of course I can garden, farm, butcher." She racked her brains. "Oh I can weave, give a neck massage… and I can do Algebra Two," she ended a bit lamely.

"I think you are overqualified," Mrs. Sanchez smiled. "But you're hired."

Madden listened in a daze as Mrs. Sanchez—please call me Luce—rattled off wages, hours, training, sick leave, and more. It rolled past Madden like a flooding arroyo as she continued to clutch Liz's hand. Reality returned somewhat as mother and daughter started chatting about accommodations.

"Liz, we could fix up the back casita. You two could share it, get you out from under my feet."

"It needs plastering, Mom."

"I can plaster," Madden murmured.

"Of course!" Liz and her mom chorused, and Madden laughed.

Someday, and soon, it would seem like an ordinary cafe. But that wasn't really true.

Because it was the start of her real life, it would always seem special to Madden.

Matteo, 2056

Something rattled. The walls of the old hotel shook. A blaring whistle rent the air and hurt Matteo's ears. Emi was sleeping soundly, despite the deafening thunder. Matteo jumped up and ran to the lobby of the hotel, then to the door. At first he thought a building had suddenly started moving. An earthquake? A bomb? Not that he'd ever experienced these things. Then his powers of observation returned. It was boxcars. One after another, a line as far as he could see, an immense line of boxcars and flatbeds and containers. Moving like a majestic snake in a long line, up a slight incline, and again that whistle seeming to break the world in half. Matteo's heart leapt. He started counting the boxcars, even though many had already passed by. 67, 68... he reached 82 before he saw the end. He was sorry not to have seen the engine.

"Take me with you," he said aloud, then felt embarrassed. It was just freight. It didn't carry people. And to go where? He was already on the move, away from Golden.

But with the train, Golden seemed to fall away. He'd left because all the GUs did was lie. He wanted to help Emi and his friends. All this made him feel good about himself.

But there was something about how the train made him feel that was the most honest. He just wanted to go. Not away, not towards. Just go.

He kept that feeling all night, because trains ran constantly through Mountainview. He'd wake up again and listen. The rattle and the whistle made him happy, so happy, despite his worry about Emi and the uncertainty of what would happen next.

Emi, 2056

In the middle of the night, Emi woke up. She was crammed against the wall, in a double bed, with Matteo heavily crushed against her.

"Move, Matteo," she hissed. "I can't breathe." And then: "Where are we?"

"You don't know? You don't remember?" He sounded worried.

"No."

"What's the last thing you do remember?"

"We were going into a town...some place?" She tried to pull it up.

"You fainted. It was hot, and you keeled over. You really don't remember?"

But she didn't. Although when Matteo explained about the store and the hotel she took it as true.

The next morning they had breakfast at the cafe with Madden. Things were moving fast. Madden explained how a cafe worked and that she had a job. She was staying.

"Liz is cute," said Emi, who'd observed her and Madden together at the store.

"Very, very cute," said Madden.

"More like OK," said Matteo.

"You idiot," Emi said. "For Madden! The woman of her dreams," she teased.

"And a good person," Madden added.

"That's obvious," Emi said.

"Isn't it!" Madden couldn't stop smiling.

But when Matteo got up to use the bathroom, Madden grabbed Emi's arm so hard it hurt. "Emi, you two are going. I'm staying. That feels terrible, but it would feel worse not to. And you're fucked up in some weird way."

"I am not," Emi said.

"OK. Whatever. But you know what I mean. And we've never been parted. Not since we were born. And we're going to have to figure this world out. And I want to see you all the time."

Matteo was back. "I have a question," Madden said, "How far from here to Albuquerque?"

"A few days walk, I think. Maybe two hours by car, you know, a truck or something. And Liz said she'd gotten us a ride. The feed store guy goes every few weeks, and he's going today. And Emi, we can look up your mom's address on this map thing, it's like on a phone."

They looked at him blankly. He continued, "but what's your mom's name?"

"Tessa. You know that."

"But her full name, like a legal name?"

"I have no idea what you're taking about. Her name is Tessa."

"Doesn't she have a last name?"

"No."

"What is Maira's last name?"

"I don't know."

But Madden had a flash. "Your grandpa. His last name is Rivers! Remember, he'd tease us and make us call him Professor Rivers when he was teaching us algebra?"

"You're a genius," Matteo said. "I'm going to get the feed store guy driver to look up Tessa Rivers on this phone map thing, and maybe we can find her."

"Oh my God," said Emi. "That's it. It was on the envelopes of the letters she sent Maira."

Matteo felt embarrassed he hadn't thought of it. Then realized it was good he hadn't said anything as he wasn't supposed to have read them.

"There is an address too?" he asked.

"Yes," Emi said.

"We can check it against this phone thing in case she's moved."

"Good," Emi said. She was starting to feel hot and dizzy again but took a few deep breaths and hoped no one would notice.

The feed store guy's truck was old and rattled in a way that was familiar and reassuring to Matteo. There was only one passenger's seat belt, so Emi strapped herself in, and Matteo sat crammed between her and the driver. He didn't mind. Being on the highway was perhaps the greatest adventure so far, better even than the drugs or the cafe or anything.

The driver was old and taciturn, like the truck. However, he did show Matteo his cell phone. It could fit in a pocket and had a tiny electronic screen. "It's pretty out of date," the old guy said. Then chuckled. "Like me. But I don't need the newest newfangled thing. It does the basics. I can check the weather. And who are you looking to visit?"

"Tessa Rivers," Matteo said.

Matteo held his breath as the guy hit some buttons.

"She's at 2814 Sweetwater Avenue SW."

"Wow!" said Matteo. "How'd you find that?"

"Look at this."

"There's a map," Matteo gasped. "Right on the phone. You can move it."

"Yup. Sonny, I think you might like Albuquerque. Too fast-paced for me, and besides, if I try and park this truck they'll slap a lot of fines on me for emissions and stuff. But you might like it."

After that, they fell into silence. The truck, despite its rattling, could do 80 miles per hour. Most cars passed it, Matteo noticed, but it still ate up the miles at an amazing rate.

The outskirts of Albuquerque were so built up that Matteo assumed this was the city itself. Then they passed the skyscrapers and bridges and whirling traffic exchanges.

Emi closed her eyes, and even Matteo, too entranced to miss a moment, felt dizzy.

The truck pulled off the highway and made a series of loopy turns. Matteo tried to memorize them but then realized there was no reason he'd ever need to retrace the route. They pulled up in front of a house that matched the address. It was bigger than any of the outbuildings at Golden, long and sprawling, built of adobe-colored frame stucco. The roof looked to be in good repair. Stop it, Matteo chided himself.

Focus.

On Emi.

On this exciting—terrifying—moment.

The old guy said good-bye, and told them to be careful. Albuquerque was a big city, full of gangs and car thieves. They thanked him and walked up a flagstone path. Emi seemed dazed, but why wouldn't she? There was a knocker, and Matteo knocked. The door opened. A woman, medium tall, not young but not old, opened it.

"Yes?" she asked them. Then her face contorted. She and Emi looked at each other.

They looked so much alike, same almond eyes, wide mouths, pointed chins. "Emi," the woman stuttered.

"Mom," Emi said. And once again she fell into a dead faint, almost cracking her head on the flagstone. Matteo only partially caught her, somewhat breaking the impact of the fall.

"Fuck," said the woman, crouching over her. Then yelled, "Paulus, get the fuck out here."

A man rushed out, moving fast but limping slightly. They picked Emi up, the woman muttering, "maybe we shouldn't move her, but fuck it," and took her into the house.

No one paid any attention to Matteo, but he followed fast. The house seemed dim compared to the light outside. The man and woman lay Emi on a couch. Fancy couch, nice carpet, Matteo noted. Nothing at Golden ever looked that clean or new.

The woman—obviously Tessa—was trying to bring Emi round. She shook her and tapped her hard. When Emi didn't respond, she tilted Emi's head back and soon was doing CPR. But Emi just lay there.

"Call 911, Paulus," Tessa ordered the man. Her voice was low and authoritative.

"What's that?" Matteo asked, but still no one paid any attention.

Almost immediately, the room was full of three burly men and women, doing all kinds of fancy things to Emi. Matteo knew some basics, but this was way beyond him.

"Her vitals are fine," one of the 911 people told Tessa. "We'll take her to UNM Hospital. She needs an MRI and more."

"No," Matteo said loudly. "Don't take her anywhere. She needs to stay with Tessa. She came all this way."

"And who the fuck might you be?" Tessa finally looked at him.

He pulled himself together and said the most convincing thing he could think of. A lie, but not a complete lie.

"I'm her husband," he said. "Her husband, Matteo, from Golden. She needs to stay here with her mother."

It took a while, but Tessa explained 911 away by saying she was some kind of special nurse, that she'd call her clinic's doctor, and to thank them, assume care and risk, etc., etc.

She covered Emi with a blanket and made some more phone calls and came back and looked hard and long at Matteo. "So Golden is into child marriage now?" she asked sarcastically.

"Tessa—you're Tessa, right? I'm sorry, I lied. We're not married, but we're kind of engaged. And we're partners. Life partners," he added, attempting to sound adult and convincing.

"OK, Matteo-life-partner. You better tell me what happened. How did you and my daughter get here?"

Paulus interjected. "Stop interrogating him, Tessa. It's obviously been a long journey. Matteo, can I get you a cold drink? A sandwich?"

Matteo looked at him gratefully and asked for an iced tea and agreed to a salami sandwich, whatever that was. It turned out to be some kind of salty cured meat—delicious. With mustard—thicker and more pungent than what he was used to. The cheese in the sandwich, though, was pale and not too flavorful.

They sat around a low table by the couch, and Matteo told his tale. If Emi had been awake to criticize him, she would have said he told it too slowly, with too much detail. Paulus seemed fascinated, though.

"So you figured out they were lying? Wow!" and "How well was the old mine shored up?"

Tessa mostly alternated between, long worried looks at Emi, prone and unresponsive, and muttering violent curses: "Fucking Golden. Evil assholes. Douche bags." Matteo didn't even know what that last one meant. And she'd break the flow of the story with worried cross-examinations about Emi.

"Could Emi be pregnant?"

"Absolutely not. She just had her period. We always use condoms."

"Does she have juvenile diabetes?"

"No," said Matteo. At least he'd never heard that.

"Has she been under stress?"

"Tessa! Listen to Matteo's story," Paulus interrupted. "Of course she's been under stress. Aren't you paying attention?"

Tessa fell silent until Matteo came to the part where Emi discovered the birthday cards and letters that Maira had kept hidden.

"Motherfucker!" Tessa yelled. She leapt up and went to the kitchen. Then the sound of plates and glasses breaking reverberated.

Matteo shot Paulus a glance. Silence emanated from the kitchen. Then a broom closet slamming and the sound of frantic sweeping and banging.

"It's OK," Paulus mouthed at Matteo. "You know, she was in the war." Matteo nodded, as if that was something he understood.

She came back and sat down. One of her fingers was bleeding, and she sucked it absent-mindedly. Matteo was coming to the part where they left Blue Arrow, when a buzzer rang, and Tessa rushed to the front door.

She admitted her boss at the clinic, Dr. Jeanette Ramos, and a stern-looking man in a turban.

"Dr. Gerald Khan, head of neurology at UNM," Dr. Ramos introduced him.

"I know your work. I'm so grateful to you both." Tessa seemed calm and gracious, not the mad woman throwing coffee mugs. "This is Emi," she gestured.

"Could she be pregnant? Seizure disorder? Diabetes? Psychosis?" Dr. Ramos was starting her intake.

"No," Tessa said definitively, as if she had raised Emi herself. "Let's go out to the garage," Paulus said to Matteo.

They went through a door off the kitchen. There in the gloom was a shining, brilliant machine, the most perfect thing Matteo had ever seen.

"What the fuck is that?" Tessa's cursing had given him permission to swear himself. He was awed. The machine gave him the feeling that a naked woman, a large joint, and a lavish dessert did, all rolled together.

"That," said Paulus softly, "is the latest, most sophisticated electric car ever made. I work on them for a living." He rattled off a sequence of numbers and letters that appeared to be the vehicle's name. "Can you drive? We'll take her out for a spin."

"I can drive," said Matteo. At that moment he forgot how he came to be talking with a stranger in a strange city, about to drive a chariot fit for the gods. "I can," he repeated, as Paulus pressed a button and opened the doors of the garage to sunlight.

Emi lay in a darkened room, unresponsive. Activity swirled around her. Tessa took a leave of absence from work and spent 24 hours a day with her, sleeping or waking.

Emi's prone body was taken to tests, scans, lab

work, MRIs, and more. Everything was normal. Physical therapists came to exercise her prone body. More doctors dropped in and out. And Emi could stay at home, because a few days in she would swallow what was put in her mouth: water, smoothies, protein drinks. Soon she'd even swallow soft food like applesauce. She lost weight, but then that leveled out. She didn't menstruate. But she did appear to dream—sometimes whimpering or even tossing a bit in her sleep.

No one knew what was wrong or how to fix it. Tessa bathed her, washed and combed her hair, changed her diapers. She was like an infant, except she neither cooed nor smiled. She did not fuss or scream or giggle.

Other people came and went. A neighbor's aunt was a curandera in Belen, and she came and smudged Emi with an egg. Reiki practitioners moved energy around with their hands. A friend of a friend knew a Pueblo healer who blew smoke. None of these people would take money for their time, so Matteo and Paulus were kept busy baking huge pies. This was one of Paulus's hobbies, and he taught Matteo, who could soon create a deliciously light crust.

They fell into a rhythm of Emi care and visitors. Paulus soon went back to work in his upscale garage and took Matteo with him. All the work on cars involved computers, and Matteo was a fast learner. They drove to work each day across a bridge over the Rio Grande. Matteo had hoped to be impressed, having never seen a great river, but it was mostly dry.

There was a Thai noodle place around the corner from the garage, and Matteo worked his way down the main dishes. They got takeout every day for lunch, and Paulus always had the same thing—Pad Thai, medium hot. At the end of two weeks, he handed Matteo a plastic card.

"What's that for?"

"Your salary. You are a big help around here. The money is on the card. You just use it to pay for things. I figured it would be easy to start with, as you don't have any bank accounts."

"I can't take money."

"Yes, you can. And this way you can start treating for lunch." Paulus smiled as Matteo accepted the plastic.

Of course Tessa had called her father, Jake, as soon as Emi arrived. He'd been worried when she'd left, and he was relieved to hear she was in Albuquerque and then worried all over again when Tessa explained what was going on.

After the kids left Jake had felt he should call Tessa and tell her. But something had held him back. Maybe it was fear of Tessa's reactions: yelling and screaming, diatribes about Golden. He figured it would work out, and he'd hear something soon.

But he couldn't come immediately. He had a few of those Golden-type commitments to honor, and he didn't want to look suspicious by vanishing. He'd be there before summer solstice.

"That's like in a month," Tessa wailed.

"Or before. Keep in touch. Let's talk every day," he said. Tessa sat back down beside Emi.

At least during these past days she hadn't thought at all about killing herself, although she was so tense the slightest sound startled her. It took her back to the time she'd been at the VA.

"You have suicidal ideation from combat trauma,"

the therapist had said the only time Tessa had gone.

In one of those arcane bureaucratic turns, Tessa was at the VA for her primary care. It turned out that although she'd thought of herself as a rebel fighting a tyrant, she had actually been legally inducted into what still considered itself the United States Army. This wasn't true of a lot of people who'd been wildcatting, but the recruiter who had signed her and the others of the Four up had indeed been official.

The therapist was a ravaged, exhausted-looking woman, a bit Tessa's senior. She had dark circles under her eyes.

"I see it all day long," she'd said wearily, and offered antidepressants. She didn't do what Tessa had expected, like ask, "How did you feel about seeing two of your closest friends blown up before your eyes?" and then Tessa would have responded, "like fucking shit," and they could have moved on.

Tessa never filled the prescription. She'd seen the therapist encode PTSD on the computer. Tessa herself often did that. It could mean anything, or nothing. It was a billing code.

Now, she turned towards Emi, who looked the same as she had looked five minutes ago. But right now Tessa didn't want to die. She wanted Emi to live.

The days passed, getting warmer. Mourning doves cooed and cottonwood trees put forth their fluff. Matteo sat in the evening holding Emi's hand. He'd feed her with a spoon. He was the one who figured out that she'd suck on a straw.

Jake came as soon as he could. He went to find Maira and at least fill her in. She'd been absent from meals since Emi had left. And he couldn't find her.

No one seemed to know where she was. And even

stranger, no one seemed to care. It was extremely odd for someone as sharp-tongued and vivid as Maira to simply slip from view in such a small community.

But Jake couldn't worry about it right now. He did extra stretching exercises and walked out a few miles to meet Tessa's car. She embraced him, sobbing.

"I'm glad to see you. Let's get going." He tossed his pack in the back and eased his game leg into the passenger's seat.

Once at Tessa's house, Jake hugged Matteo, who clutched him fiercely. They'd be sharing a room that was usually Jake's, but Jake reassured him it was fine.

And there was Emi, stretched out thin and pale beneath a soft white blanket. Jake went up to her and touched her shoulder and said, "Wake up, Emi. It's Jake. Your grandpa. I'm here. Wake up."

Emi opened her eyes and took his hand. "Hi Grandpa," she said weakly. "How come you're here?"

"I was worried about you. Can you sit up?"

She nodded, and he propped her against the pillows. She felt safe in his big arms. "Am I... like, at my mom's?"

"Yup."

"Matteo?"

"He's in the kitchen."

"Baking? Sometimes I'd hear them talking."

"Waiting for you to wake up, honey."

"I'm waking up," she said.

Tessa had been standing stock-still, staring at her father. "Hey," she called to Paulus and Matteo in a shell-shocked tone. "Come in here."

It was Paulus, of all of them, who burst into tears that he couldn't stop flowing.

Maira, 2056

Maira sat up all night. The girl was feverish, tossing and turning. She moaned softly, making unaccustomed sounds. At dawn, both of them dozed. Maira dreamed that she was back in Vegas, so long ago. She was inside the huge pyramid of black glass. It was empty of people. Trees had grown up, and plants had split their pots. Brightly colored birds flitted about, twittering. It was lush, a jungle, but she couldn't find the source of water. Outside, she could tell, the sky was dry and brilliant. There were no clouds, not day or night. She walked past a bathroom and saw that all the automatic faucets were on and the sinks were overflowing.

Water streamed out and filled the corridors with rivulets. Now she was following along the edge of the pyramid, with the rows of hotel rooms, each with slanted walls. She opened one just by touching the door knob. She had no key. She went in. The window showed a night sky, dazzling, like a painting of comets and meteors and ringed planets. An old woman was sitting on the neatly made guest bed. She was older than Maira and looked very old-fashioned. She was wearing a faded cotton dress and an apron. Oddly, the top of the dress was fastened with a beautiful golden brooch in the shape of the sun.

"I'd get out of here if I were you," the old woman told her.

Maira woke with a start. She touched the girl's forehead. It was cool. The fever had broken. Maira offered her some water in a glass with a bent straw. The girl drank deeply. And so Maira continued to care for the girl.

Every so often, Maira would a take a break and go for a soak late at night when no one else was around. She floated in the pond, naked. The warm spring gushed faithfully, and the water was a pleasant temperature.

Maira lay on her back and looked at the stars. Had they always been in those positions, those constellations? Somehow they looked different, as if they had changed. She looked for the North Star, but couldn't locate it.

Still, she floated at her leisure. Time enough to soak before she got out, dried off, and went back to tending Emi.

Emi, 2056-2066

Life went on its way. Things that had seemed incomprehensible, and marvelous, became pleasant and ordinary. Emi recovered. She and Matteo got married in a small ceremony in Tessa's backyard. Of course Madden and Co came, along with their partners. Guests included Liz's mom, Crystal's family, and Dr. Ramos. Emi wore the silver earrings she'd filched from Maira's drawer so long ago. She got a lot of compliments and said she'd been lucky to find them at a flea market.

Matteo went to work for Paulus and then to technical college. Soon he was a software expert working on his own. He was so good, and the money flowed.

Sometimes he could be awkward with a client, either saying too much or staring blankly. But Emi coached him. They'd never fit in perfectly in Albuquerque, but they were making a go of it. She went to UNM and got a nursing degree and went to work in a cardiac unit. Tessa was proud of her, although she tried to get Emi more interested in general public health. But Emi liked working with hearts. She was interested in broken-heart syndrome but also the more run-of-the-mill problems.

They bought a little house a few blocks from Tessa and Paulus. They'd sit out every Sunday night that it was warm enough—which was increasingly most of the time—and barbecue and play cards. Matteo always won, unless they ganged up on him. On weekends they went to the growers' markets and craft fairs. Emi had started wearing jewelry, and she bought Tessa things too. Tessa often wore the funky, chunky plastic bracelets Emi had got her, as well as the fine Navajo piece of an inlaid turquoise butterfly. However, once Emi bought her a little pin of a hand holding a pink heart. And Tessa never wore that.

Matteo and Emi had two children... first Noah and then Cora. Emi loved their names but was surprised when she enrolled Noah in preschool to find at least four other boys in his class with the same name. It was as if the parents were expecting a disaster, maybe a huge flood instead of all this drought, and had named their children to stay afloat.

Then Madden and Liz had two children—one each. Emi tried to pry about who the fathers were—or father, once Madden let drop that it was the same guy. She just said "turkey baster" and laughed and laughed. Emi laughed as well. It was impossible to get anything out of Madden that she didn't want to share. The two little girls were close in age and looked alike.

Co and David broke up. Co said it was mutual and that they were friends. Then at the next gathering Co showed up with a very tough and very chic redheaded woman. They held hands and looked at each other adoringly.

"So Co is now a lesbian?" Emi was never content to let this topic rest.

"Leave Co alone," said Matteo.

"I'm not sure this redhead is gay," Madden said.

"Then what?" Emi insisted.

"Just a knockout who loves Co?" Madden ventured.

"Leave Co alone," Matteo said again.

"Of course," Emi agreed. "Co is doing great."

Co had become a composer and a conductor, working first with community orchestras and then commissions. Co's music was evocative and strange, with lots of percussion, sometimes even wind chimes. At times it was lulling, seeming to go on and on in endless fashion, then suddenly becoming almost danceable. Critics loved it, although sometimes old fogies in the audience walked out.

Co did seem very happy, as did the fashionable redhead. Everyone seemed content with life. Except for Emi.

Tessa noticed first. Emi looked pale. Tessa checked—her pulse was a little fast. She seemed to be eating less, losing weight. Tessa suggested she get some tests, but Emi just shook her head. "I'm fine, mom," she'd say. "Stop worrying."

But Tessa couldn't stop worrying. She took Matteo to coffee and fussed at him. He had no idea what to do. The truth was, Emi seemed fine to him. She'd recovered from fainting that time in Mountainview and her near-coma or whatever it was when they arrived in Albuquerque. She was strong. They were busy. He was completely happy when they were in bed together. She smelled of the past—a twinge of dust and pine—and tasted like the future, something unknown and mysterious. He loved her. It was not in his nature to worry too much until he knew what he was worried about.

Still, he gave in to Tessa. Paulus would babysit. He and Emi would have dinner with Tessa, ostensibly to talk about making some legal changes to her house's ownership, joint tenancy, some made-up issues. They went to Yanni's. It was still warm enough to sit on the enclosed patio although it was almost December.

They'd no sooner ordered a big platter of appetizers than Tessa launched into Emi. Something was wrong. What was it? What was Emi hiding?

"I'm not...hiding...anything," Emi said, focusing for a moment on some kalamata olives, then spitting out the pits. And then she added carefully, "But I am upset about something."

"What? Is it your health?" Tessa had her pit bull act going. Sometimes Matteo wondered if it was because she hadn't taken care of Emi much when she was a baby. All that tender care and concern and hovering was thrust on her adult daughter. A competent person, he added to himself. A woman who didn't need to be fussed over.

"I'm worried about Maira," Emi said.

Both Matteo and Tessa just stared at her. Matteo said "What?"

Tessa said. "Fuck Maira. Just fucking fuck her."

"No," said Emi. "She raised me." Tessa's face fell. "Not your fault, Mom. But she did. She was my mom and grandma rolled into one. She protected me, cared for me. I don't think I realized until we had our own kids. She did a lot, everything."

Tessa nodded.

"And, Mom, I just left her. We walked out in the middle of the night. I even took her money. I must have broken her heart."

"She lied," Matteo said.

"Oh come off it. You always harp on that. Sure, the GUs lied. Look, even Jake lied, but we aren't mad at him now. And Matteo, you always think we left because they lied. But that really isn't true. I left to find Tessa. Madden left to fall in love. Co left to be Co. This wasn't about lying. This was about growing up, trying to be free, to find our own ways."

"OK," Matteo said. "I can agree. But for me the lying was a big part of it."

"I want to go back," Emi said. "To visit Golden. To apologize to Maira. To introduce my kids to her."

"Is that safe?" Tessa asked.

"For God's sake, Mom. Of course it is. It is probably safer than walking out in the parking lot here behind Yanni's! What are they gonna do? Hold us captive? Brainwash us? We have phones, cars. We'll check it with Jake. Heck, we can always walk out again."

Matteo smiled, pleased by the image...his kids trooping along.

"Do you need to borrow a gun? Swear to me that this will be just a visit," Tessa said.

"You know, you could come with us," Emi murmured.

"No thank you. Never. Fucking never. Just swear."

"I swear," said Emi. "I swear on these delicious Greek appetizers. And I don't need a ridiculous gun."

"Guns aren't ridiculous. Swear seriously."

"Seriously. I'm coming back. We all will." Emi said.

"OK," said Tessa. She smeared some baba ghanoush on a slice of pita bread. "I believe you. Mostly."

"We're going close to Blue Arrow," Matteo had said to Emi. "Are you curious to see what's still there, what it looks like now?"

"Sort of...you decide," she told him. Once they'd agreed to go to Golden, she wanted to go as quickly as possible. Except for the part of her that wanted to put it off.

Late afternoon, winter leaning towards spring, the quiet road, both kids napping peacefully in the back seats. Blue Arrow was just a few minutes off their route. Matteo had checked the maps on his phone. Something was still there.

They pulled off into the ruins of a parking lot... buckled asphalt, tumbleweeds, and crows. The big arrow was still there, but just the frame. It was a haunted structure; you could see right through it.

They got out of the car, leaving the windows rolled down in case the kids woke up. And looked at the ruins of the old motel, more decrepit even than when they had last seen it.

The wind whistled. There was no other building. The place that they both remembered as having hot springs, as being called "The Ziggurat," was completely empty.

"Where was it? The bathhouse? Was that even real?" Emi asked.

"It certainly was real," Matteo said. "Real things happened here."

"You were tripping."

"Yes. But I vividly remember before and after. Being in the water. And you and Madden heading off for adventure."

"Yeah."

"It just must have... gone somewhere else."

They turned back towards the car, looking at the empty swimming pool, bleached and cracked. The metal staircases had corroded and fallen.

Then Emi heard music. It was a bit like what Co wrote, only more rhythmic... maybe marimbas. It went on for a long minute. Emi lifted her chin to the sky, entranced.

"What?"

"You don't hear music?"

"No," Matteo said. "Well, almost. But not really."

"It's over now," Emi said.

They got back in the car.

"Do you think Golden might be gone too?" she asked.

"Of course not. Jake still lives there."

"Sometimes things disappear."

"It's on the map, Emi. Buildings, machinery, everything."

"A map isn't real," she said.

He wanted to argue with her, but instead he turned the car on and headed out. The kids were still sleeping.

By the time they pulled into the grid of rural roads near Golden, the kids were awake. They'd peed in bushes, eaten somewhat unhealthy snacks that had been brought along as a treat, and were now watching a movie. A few hours in a car with kids, Matteo mused, could feel like a lifetime. Well, they could run around and let off steam at Golden. There'd be kids there. Kids of people he'd known as kids. He checked himself for some soft sentimental feeling about Golden but couldn't find it. He himself had no need to go back. He was doing it for Emi, trusting that she knew something that would be best for all of them.

"We're just going to park and walk in?"

"That's the plan," he said.

He pulled over to the shoulder of the dirt road and they got out. He resisted the urge to hide the vehicle under weeds and branches. So maybe he did have some feelings about Golden after all. Fear. "I'm a grown-up," Matteo reminded himself. For a moment he wished that Jake would also be there at Golden to meet up with them. But of course Jake was hiding out at Tessa's, not wanting to blow his cover. How could Jake pretend he didn't know Emi in Albuquerque, let alone his great-grandchildren? It was way too complicated, too many layers of lies, to pull off.

Matteo and Emi looked around. There was an overgrown track that should lead to Golden. Of course they hadn't come out this way when they'd left; they'd come through the mine. They looked around.

"The sign's gone," Emi said.

"There was a sign?"

"Of course. We saw it when we were kids. A baby riding on a horse. With the rays of the sun."

"I don't remember," Matteo said.

"A baby?" Cora piped up. "Where is the mommy? Where is the daddy?"

"Good question," Emi muttered.

"Is the baby all alone?"

"The baby is fine," Emi snapped. Cora was at that age when everything was in groups. Emi had told her... not every baby has one mommy and one daddy. Some people have two mommies. Some babies....

But this fell on deaf ears.

"I don't see a baby," said Noah, the literalist.

"Kids! Start walking."

"Is it a long walk?" from Noah.

"No. Short. Very short. Emi wants to see her grandma."

"My gran-ma is in Burque," Cora added.

"Yes. But Mommy's grandma is here. Start walking. No whining." As always, Matteo could be focused, Emi thought, which was good. She might just have stood out in the sun discussing babies. Now that they were so close, it was an effort to force her legs to move her even closer.

But move they did, ten minutes along the overgrown path.

And there was Golden, as if they'd never left. A cluster of buildings, most in pretty good repair, Matteo noted. "New water catchment system," he said, but no one was listening.

"Chickens!" Cora said.

"Look at that climbing structure!" said Noah, precise as always.

Emi stood stunned. There was wind, dust, the smell of bread baking and manure, the sound of trees and maybe of water bubbling up from underground, of little animals burrowing. Then everything went totally still. Then the sky rang as if it was a gong hit with a mallet.

"Emi." Matteo touched her shoulder, and everything returned to normal.

"Can I help you?" A pretty, frazzled-looking woman with a baby on her hip was standing in front of them. "We don't allow drop-in visitors here. Are you lost? I can offer you some water, but that's all."

"Sarah," Emi said. "It's us."

"Emi?"

"Yes."

"You still can't stay here. You left. You can't just come back."

"Why would we want to come back?" Matteo burst out. "You know, Sarah, I was right. The world is still there. A huge, enormous world full of amazing things. It didn't end. They just lied and lied to us. Emi's mom is alive. Madden fell in love with a beautiful woman, Liz. They have two kids and a cool store. She's fine. We have good jobs and a nice house."

Sarah scoffed. "We know they lied. And we'll lie too. Who do you think does the town tripping now? Us, of course. But childhood should be innocent."

"Oh, so does the Easter Bunny live here now? Where is Santa Claus?"

Sarah looked like she was about to spit. But Emi interrupted. "I've come to see Maira. Where is she? I've come to see her."

"Maira?"

"Yes, my grandmother, Maira. You might have heard of her? Where the fuck is she?"

"Maira?"

"Is there a problem?" A tall, sun-scorched man appeared behind Sarah. Akira just looked like an old, slightly burnt-out version of himself.

"Matteo. Emi." He'd recognized them at once.

"I want to see Maira. Where is she?"

"Around... somewhere."

"Get her now," Emi said.

"Dad," Noah interrupted, "can I go play? Climb? There are some kids there."

"Absolutely not." Matteo grabbed his son's hand.

"Is Maira sick?" Emi asked.

"She's sort of a recluse. She lives in one of the outbuildings. Eats alone."

"Well, I'm glad Golden is taking good care of an old lady," Emi snapped. "Go and tell her I'm here."

"I'll get her," Akira said. Sarah shot Emi a look of pure hate. She didn't offer them a drink again. Instead, she turned and strode off. Matteo commandeered a picnic table, and started handing out snacks from his backpack.

The kids looked shell-shocked.

"The lady was mean," Cora said.

"Yes," Emi said. "They are mean."

"Can I...." Noah tried again.

"Nobody is moving from this table," Matteo said. "Mom is going to say hi to her grandma and then we're leaving. In ten minutes. Sit still."

But Maira did not appear. Instead, a stocky, bearded guy came around from the kitchen with a tray with glasses and a jug of lemonade.

"Hi," he said.

Matteo could not place the guy by looks, but the voice was familiar. "Liam?" he said.

"The same." Liam smiled and started pouring lemonade for everyone. "Matteo. Emi. You look good. Cute kids! Are you back for a visit?"

"Emi wants to see Maira," Matteo said.

"Cool. I think Sarah went to get her."

"And Akira and Sarah have been pretty rude."

"Yeah," said Liam. "They are really uptight. But you know, it is fine for you to visit. There is no policy about that anymore. It was rough after you four left. Pretty lonely. But Golden has loosened up. My wife, Tina, she actually came to visit and decided to stay," he shrugged. "Which was good, because I could never get any woman from Golden interested in me." He laughed. "And you two are still together! I'm not surprised. Madden is OK? How is Co?"

Emi said, "Co is a famous musician and composer," in her mostly prickly voice.

"Nice," said Liam, in a vague manner. Then turning to Matteo, "Hey, you wouldn't believe the improvements we've made with the solar."

And before he could remember to resist, Matteo was chatting away with Liam.

Emi was annoyed, but she focused on her lemonade, which really was delicious.

At that moment, a very old-looking woman came tentatively around the corner, headed towards them. Her gait was unsteady and her eyes squinted, even against the pale sun.

"Maira," Emi said. "It's me, it's me. It's Emi. I've come back. To apologize for leaving the way I did. To say I love you. To check on you. And I want you to meet my children. This is Noah, and the girl is Cora. They are your great-grandchildren!"

The old woman peered at her. "Emi?"

"Yes. It's me."

"But you have nothing to apologize for. You've been here the whole time."

"What? No, I've been in Albuquerque."

"You've been right here. Sick in bed. You can't talk, but you can understand. I've been taking care of you."

"No, no."

Then they all saw the figure, a young woman in a nightgown, walk slowly towards them. Matteo never discussed it with the kids. But he was sure they saw what he did.

The woman was barefoot. And transparent. Sunshine and grass and trees were visible right through her. Light seemed to intensify around her and the air was golden. She didn't speak. She just came towards Emi, closer and closer. Emi stood completely still.

And then they merged into each other and became one person. "Mommy," Cora said, in a severe voice.

"Yes. It's me," Emi answered.

Tessa, 2056

"It's almost dinnertime," Jake said to Tessa. They were sitting out in the dusk. She gave a shudder.

"Are you cold?" he asked.

"No, I just felt kind of weird for a moment. Kind of... weird, I don't know."

"Better or worse?" Jake was always analytic.

"Oh Dad, I don't know." Just as if something I'd lost had come back, she thought. But hadn't that already happened?

Her phone chimed a text. "It's the kids," she told him. "Matteo says they're fine, halfway home already. It went OK with Maira. Emi's satisfied."

He smiled at her. "I'm sure I'll get a full story back at Golden."

"You're still going back tomorrow? You don't want to stay longer? I love having you here. Oh Dad, consider moving? We're all here."

"You know I love Golden," he said. "It's my home."

"I know you love it. I don't really know why, though."

He shot her a glance.

"Well, it's good enough for me if you love it." Tessa retreated. "So what do you want for dinner? There's that new pan-Asian place. Paulus likes the Old Lady Dofu. We could get Thai-style spicy eggplant. Should I get some sushi appetizers?"

"Sounds good," Jake said. "And a side of noodles. With everything."

Miriam Sagan is the author of over thirty books of poetry, fiction, and memoir. These include *Border Line* (Cholla Needles, 2022), *Shadow on the Minotaur* (Red Mountain, 2020), and *Star Gazing* (Cholla Needles, 2020). She has been a writer in residence in four national parks, Yaddo, MacDowell, Gulkistan in Iceland, Kura Studio in Japan, and other interesting and remote places. She founded and directed the creative writing program at Santa Fe Community College. She works as part of the intergeneration collaborative team Maternal Mitochondria (with Isabel Winson-Sagan) which has produced text installations in venues ranging from abandoned buildings to galleries to RV parks. Her work has been incised on stoneware as part of two haiku pathways, set to music for the Santa Fe Women's Ensemble, and left in Little Free Libraries across the country.

Made in the USA
Coppell, TX
24 March 2024